The Book of Ghosts

selected and illustrated by **Michael Hague** and **Devon Hague**

HarperCollins*Publishers*

Other books selected and illustrated by Michael Hague

The Book of Fairy Poetry

The Book of Pirates

The Book of Fairies

The Book of Dragons

The Book of Wizards

To Maddy

—M.H. & D.H.

The Book of Ghosts
Copyright © 2009 by Michael Hague
All rights reserved. Manufactured in China.
No part of this book may be used or reproduced in any manner whatsoever without written permission except in the case of
brief quotations embodied in critical articles and reviews. For information address HarperCollins Children's Books,
a division of HarperCollins Publishers, 1350 Avenue of the Americas, New York, NY 10019.
www.harpercollinschildrens.com

Library of Congress Cataloging-in-Publication Data
The book of ghosts / selected and illustrated by Michael Hague and Devon Hague. — 1st ed.
  v. cm.
  Contents: The legend of Sleepy Hollow / Washington Irving – The tell-tale heart / Edgar Allan Poe — The mummy's curse / Louisa
May Alcott — The Canterville ghost / Oscar Wilde — The monkey's paw / W. W. Jacobs — The story of the inexperienced ghost
/ H. G. Wells – A diagnosis of death / Ambrose Bierce — Laura / adapted from Saki (H. H.Munro) — The statement of Randolph
Carter / from H. P. Lovecraft.
  ISBN 978-0-688-14008-3 (trade bdg.)
  1. Ghost stories, American. 2. Ghost stories, English. 3. Horror tales, American. 4. Horror tales, English. [1. Ghosts—Fiction.
2. Horror stories. 3. Short stories.] I. Hague, Michael, ill. II. Hague, Devon, ill.
PZ5.B6426 2009   2008013855
[Fic]—dc22   CIP
                                                                                                                          AC

Typography by Jeanne L. Hogle
1 2 3 4 5 6 7 8 9 10

First Edition

Contents

THE LEGEND OF SLEEPY HOLLOW
ADAPTED FROM WASHINGTON IRVING
9

THE TELL~TALE HEART
ADAPTED FROM EDGAR ALLAN POE
35

THE MUMMY'S CURSE
ADAPTED FROM LOUISA MAY ALCOTT
45

THE CANTERVILLE GHOST
ADAPTED FROM OSCAR WILDE
61

THE MONKEY'S PAW
ADAPTED FROM W. W. JACOBS
79

THE STORY OF THE INEXPERIENCED GHOST
ADAPTED FROM H. G. WELLS
95

A DIAGNOSIS OF DEATH
ADAPTED FROM AMBROSE BIERCE
115

LAURA
ADAPTED FROM SAKI (H. H. MUNRO)
123

THE STATEMENT OF RANDOLPH CARTER
ADAPTED FROM H. P. LOVECRAFT
131

chapter 1

THE LEGEND OF SLEEPY HOLLOW

ADAPTED FROM WASHINGTON IRVING

In the bosom of one of those spacious coves which indent the eastern shore of the Hudson, at that broad expansion of the river denominated by the ancient Dutch navigators the Tappan Zee, and where they always prudently shortened sail and implored the protection of St. Nicholas when they crossed, there lies a small market town or rural port, which by some is called Greensburgh, but which is more generally and properly known by the name of Tarry Town. This name was given, we are told, in former days, by the good housewives of the adjacent country, from the inveterate propensity of their husbands to linger about the village tavern on market days. Be that as it may, I do not vouch for the fact, but merely advert to it, for the sake of being precise and authentic. Not far from this village, perhaps about two miles, there is a little valley or rather lap of land among high hills, which is one of the quietest places in the whole world. A small brook glides through it, with just murmur enough to lull one to repose; and the occasional whistle of a quail or tapping of a woodpecker is almost the only sound that ever breaks in upon the uniform tranquility.

From the listless repose of the place, and the peculiar character of its inhabitants, who are descendants from the original Dutch settlers, this sequestered glen has long been known by the name of Sleepy Hollow, and its rustic lads are called the Sleepy Hollow Boys throughout all the neighboring country. A drowsy, dreamy influence seems to hang over the land, and to pervade the very atmosphere. Some say that the place was bewitched by a High German doctor, during the early days of the settlement; others, that an old Indian chief, the prophet or wizard of his tribe, held his powwows there before the country was discovered by Master Hendrick Hudson. Certain it is, the place still continues under the sway of some witching power that holds a spell over the minds of the good people, causing them to walk in a continual reverie. They are given to all kinds of marvelous beliefs, are subject to trances and visions, and frequently see strange sights, and hear music and voices in the air. The whole neighborhood abounds with local tales, haunted spots, and twilight superstitions; stars shoot and meteors glare oftener across the valley than in any other part of the country, and the nightmare, with her whole herd, seems to make it the favorite scene of her gambols.

The dominant spirit, however, that haunts this enchanted region, and seems to be commander-in-chief of all the powers of the air, is the apparition of a figure on horseback, without a head. It is said by some to be the ghost of a Hessian trooper, whose head had been carried away by a cannon-ball, in some nameless battle during the Revolutionary War, and who is ever and anon seen by the country folk hurrying along in the gloom of night, as if on the wings of the wind. His haunts are not confined to the valley, but extend at times to the adjacent roads, and especially to the vicinity of a church at no great distance. Indeed, certain of the most authentic historians of those parts, who have been careful in collecting and collating the floating facts concerning this specter, allege that the body of the trooper having been buried in the churchyard, the ghost rides forth to the scene of battle in nightly quest of his head, and that the rushing speed with which he sometimes passes along the Hollow, like a midnight blast, is owing to his being belated, and in a hurry to get back to the churchyard before daybreak. Such is the general purport of this legendary superstition, which has furnished materials for many a wild story in that region of shadows; and the specter is known at all the country firesides, by the name of the Headless Horseman of Sleepy Hollow.

In this by-place of nature there abode, in a remote period of American history, that is to say, some thirty years since, a worthy fellow of the name of Ichabod Crane, who sojourned, or, as he expressed it, "tarried," in Sleepy Hollow, for the purpose of instructing the children of the vicinity. The last name of Crane was not inapplicable to his person. He was tall, but exceedingly lank, with narrow shoulders, long arms and legs, hands that dangled a mile out of his sleeves, feet that might have served for shovels, and his whole frame most loosely hung together. His head was small, and flat at top, with huge ears, large green glassy eyes, and a long snipe nose, so that it looked like a weathercock perched upon his spindle neck to tell which way the wind blew. To see him striding along the profile of a hill on a windy day, with his clothes bagging and

fluttering about him, one might have mistaken him for the genius of famine descending upon the earth, or some scarecrow eloped from a cornfield.

His schoolhouse was a low building of one large room, rudely constructed of logs; the windows partly glazed, and partly patched with leaves of old copybooks. The schoolhouse stood in a rather lonely but pleasant situation, just at the foot of a woody hill, with a brook running close by, and a formidable birch-tree growing at one end of it. From hence the low murmur of his pupils' voices, conning over their lessons, might be heard in a drowsy summer's day, like the hum of a beehive; interrupted now and then by the authoritative voice of the master, in the tone of menace or command, or, peradventure, by the appalling sound of the birch, as he urged some tardy loiterer along the flowery path of knowledge. Truth to say, he was a conscientious man, and ever bore in mind the golden maxim "Spare the rod and spoil the child." Ichabod Crane's scholars certainly were not spoiled.

The schoolmaster is generally a man of some importance in the female circle of a rural neighborhood; being considered a kind of idle, gentlemanlike personage, of vastly superior taste and accomplishments to the rough country swains, and, indeed, inferior in learning only to the parson. His appearance, therefore, is apt to occasion some little stir at the tea-table of a farmhouse, and the addition of a supernumerary dish of cakes or sweetmeats, or, peradventure, the parade of a silver teapot. Our man of letters, therefore, was peculiarly happy in the smiles of all the country damsels. How he would figure among them in the churchyard, between services on Sundays; gathering grapes for them from the wild vines that overran the surrounding trees; reciting for their amusement all the epitaphs on the tombstones; or sauntering, with a whole bevy of them, along the banks of the adjacent millpond; while the more bashful country bumpkins hung sheepishly back, envying his superior elegance and address.

From his half-itinerant life, also, he was a kind of traveling gazette, carrying the whole catalog of local gossip from house to house, so that his appearance was always greeted with satisfaction. He was, moreover, esteemed by the women as a man of great erudition, for he had read several books quite through, and was a perfect master of Cotton Mather's *History of New England Witchcraft*, in which, by the way, he most firmly and potently believed.

He was, in fact, an odd mixture of small shrewdness and simple credulity.

His appetite for the marvelous, and his powers of digesting it, were equally extraordinary; and both had been increased by his residence in this spell-bound region. No tale was too gross or monstrous for his capacious swallow. It was often his delight, after his school was dismissed in the afternoon, to stretch himself on the rich bed of clover bordering the little brook that whimpered by his schoolhouse, and there read over old Mather's direful tales, until the gathering dusk of evening made the printed page a mere mist before his eyes. Then, as he wended his way by swamp and stream and awful woodland, to the farmhouse where he happened to be quartered, every sound of nature, at that witching hour, fluttered his excited imagination,—the moan of the whip-poor-will from the hillside, the boding cry of the tree toad, that harbinger of storm, the dreary hooting of the screech owl, or the sudden rustling in the thicket of birds frightened from their roost. The fireflies, too, which sparkled most vividly in the darkest places, now and then startled him, as one of un-common brightness would stream across his path; and if, by chance, a huge blockhead of a beetle came winging his blundering flight against him, the poor varlet was ready to give up the ghost, with the idea that he was struck with a witch's token. His only resource on such occasions, either to drown thought or drive away evil spirits, was to sing psalm tunes; and the good people of Sleepy Hollow, as they sat by their doors of an evening, were often filled with awe at hearing his nasal melody, "in linked sweetness long drawn out," floating from the distant hill, or along the dusky road.

Another of his sources of fearful pleasure was to pass long winter evenings with the old Dutch wives, as they sat spinning by the fire, with a row of apples roasting and spluttering along the hearth, and listen to their marvelous tales of ghosts and goblins, and haunted fields, and haunted brooks, and haunted bridges, and haunted houses, and particularly of the Headless Horseman, or Galloping Hessian of the Hollow, as they sometimes called him.

All these, however, were mere terrors of the night, phantoms of the mind that walk in darkness; and though he had seen many specters in his time, and been more than once beset by Satan in diverse shapes, in his lonely perambulations, yet daylight put an end to all these evils; and he would have passed a pleasant life of it, in spite of the Devil and all his works, if his path had not been crossed by a being that causes more perplexity to mortal man than ghosts, goblins, and the whole race of witches put together, and that was—a woman.

Among the musical disciples who assembled, one evening in each week, to receive his instructions in psalmody, was Katrina Van Tassel, the daughter and only child of a substantial Dutch farmer. She was a blooming lass of fresh eighteen; plump as a partridge; ripe and melting and rosy-cheeked as one of her father's peaches, and universally famed, not merely for her beauty, but her vast expectations. She was withal a little of a coquette, as might be perceived even in her dress, which was a mixture of ancient and modern fashions, as most suited to set off her charms. She wore clothes of imported silk; the tempting stomacher of the olden time, and withal a provokingly short petticoat, to display the prettiest foot and ankle in the country round.

Ichabod Crane had a soft and foolish heart toward the sex; and it is not to be wondered at that so tempting a morsel soon found favor in his eyes, more especially after he had visited her in her paternal mansion. Old Baltus Van

Tassel was a perfect picture of a thriving, contented, liberal-hearted farmer. His stronghold was situated on the banks of the Hudson, in one of those green, sheltered, fertile nooks in which the Dutch farmers are so fond of nestling. Hard by the farmhouse was a vast barn that might have served for a church, every window and crevice of which seemed bursting forth with the treasures of the farm; sleek unwieldy porkers were grunting in the repose and abundance of their pens, from whence sallied forth, now and then, troops of suckling pigs, as if to snuff the air. A stately squadron of snowy geese were riding in an adjoining pond, convoying whole fleets of ducks; regiments of turkeys were gobbling through the farmyard, and Guinea fowls fretting about it, like ill-tempered housewives, with their peevish, discontented cry.

The pedagogue's mouth watered as he looked upon this sumptuous promise of luxurious winter fare. In his devouring mind's eye, he pictured to himself every roasting pig running about with a pudding in his belly, and an apple in his mouth; the geese were swimming in their own gravy; and the ducks pairing cosily in dishes, like snug married couples, with a decent competency of onion sauce. In the porkers he saw carved out the future sleek side of bacon, and juicy relishing ham; not a turkey but he beheld daintily trussed up, with its gizzard under its wing, and, peradventure, a necklace of savory sausages.

As the enraptured Ichabod fancied all this, and as he rolled his great green eyes over the fat meadowlands, the rich fields of wheat, of rye, of buckwheat, and Indian corn, and the orchards burdened with ruddy fruit, which surrounded the warm tenement of Van Tassel, his heart yearned after the damsel who was to inherit these domains. When he entered the house, the conquest of his heart was complete. It was one of those spacious farmhouses, with high-ridged but lowly sloping roofs, built in the style handed down from the first Dutch settlers; the low projecting eaves forming a piazza along the front, capable of being closed up in bad weather. From here the wondering Ichabod entered the hall, which formed the center of the mansion, and the place of usual residence. Here rows of resplendent pewter, ranged on a long dresser, dazzled his eyes. In one corner stood a huge bag of wool, ready to be spun; in another, a quantity of linsey-woolsey just from the loom; ears of Indian corn, and strings of dried apples and peaches, hung in gay festoons along the walls, mingled with the gaud of red peppers; and a door left ajar gave him a peep into the best parlor, where the claw-footed chairs and dark mahogany tables shone like mirrors; and a corner cupboard, knowingly left open, displayed immense treasures of old silver and well-mended china.

From the moment Ichabod laid his eyes upon these regions of delight, the peace of his mind was at an end, and his only study was how to gain the affections of the peerless daughter of Van Tassel. In this enterprise, however, he had more real difficulties than generally fell to the lot of a knight-errant of yore, who seldom had anything but giants, enchanters, fiery dragons, and suchlike easily conquered adversaries, to contend with. Ichabod, on the contrary, had to win his way to the heart of a country coquette, beset with a labyrinth of whims and caprices, which were forever presenting new difficulties and impediments; and he had to encounter a host of fearful adversaries of real flesh and blood, the numerous rustic admirers, who beset every portal to her heart, keeping a watchful and angry eye upon each other, but ready to fly out in the common cause against any new competitor.

Among these, the most formidable was a burly, roaring, roistering blade, of the name of Abraham, or, according to the Dutch abbreviation, Brom Van Brunt, the hero of the country round, which rang with his feats of strength and hardihood. He was broad-shouldered and double-jointed, with short curly black hair, and a bluff but not unpleasant countenance, having a mingled air of fun and arrogance. From his Herculean frame and great powers of limb he had received the nickname of Brom Bones, by which he was universally known. He was famed for great knowledge and skill in horsemanship, being as dexterous on horseback as a Tartar. He was foremost at all races and cockfights; and was always ready for either a fight or a frolic; but had more mischief than ill-will in his composition. With all his overbearing roughness, there was a strong dash of waggish good humor at bottom. The neighbors looked upon him with a mixture of awe, admiration, and good-will; and, when any madcap prank or rustic brawl occurred in the vicinity, always shook their heads, and warranted Brom Bones was at the bottom of it.

This rustic hero had for some time singled out the blooming Katrina for the object of his uncouth gallantries, and though his amorous toyings were something like the gentle caresses and endearments of a bear, yet it was whispered that she did not altogether discourage his hopes. Such was the formidable rival with whom Ichabod Crane had to contend, and, considering all things, a stouter man than he would have shrunk from the competition, and a wiser man would have despaired. To have taken the field openly against his rival would have been madness; for he was not a man to be thwarted in his amours, any more than that stormy lover Achilles. Ichabod, therefore, made his advances in a quiet and gently insinuating manner. Under cover of his character of singing master, he made frequent visits at the farmhouse and would carry on his suit with the lass by the side of the spring under the great elm, or sauntering along in the twilight, that hour so favorable to the lover's eloquence. Brom, who had a degree of rough chivalry in his nature, would fain have carried matters to open warfare and have settled their pretensions to the lady, according to the mode of those most concise and simple reasoners, the knights-errant of yore,—by single combat; but Ichabod was too conscious of the superior might of his adversary to enter the lists against him.

On a fine autumnal afternoon, Ichabod sat enthroned on the lofty stool from whence he usually watched all the concerns of his little pedagogical realm when a messenger came clattering up to the school door with an invitation to Ichabod to attend a merry-making or "quilting frolic," to be held that evening at Mynheer Van Tassel's. The gallant Ichabod then spent at least an extra half hour at his toilet, brushing and furbishing up his best and indeed only suit, and arranging his locks by a bit of broken looking glass that hung up in the schoolhouse. That he might make his appearance before his mistress in the true style of a cavalier, he borrowed a horse from the farmer with whom he boarded, a choleric old Dutchman of the name of Hans Van Ripper, and, thus gallantly mounted, issued forth like a knight-errant in quest of adventures. But it is meet I should, in the true spirit of romantic story, give some account of the looks and equipments of my hero and his steed. The animal he bestrode was a broken-down plow horse that had outlived almost everything but its viciousness. He was gaunt and shagged, with a ewe neck, and a head like a hammer; his rusty mane and tail were tangled and knotted with burrs; one eye had lost its pupil, and was glaring and spectral, but the other had the gleam of a genuine devil in it. Still he must have had fire and mettle in his day, if we may judge from the name he bore of Gunpowder. He had, in fact, been a favorite steed of his master's, the choleric Van Ripper, who was a furious rider, and had infused, very probably, some of his own spirit into the animal; for, old and broken-down as he looked, there was more of the lurking devil in him than in any young filly in the country.

Ichabod was a suitable figure for such a steed. He rode with short stirrups, which brought his knees nearly up to the pommel of the saddle; his sharp elbows stuck out like grasshoppers'; he carried his whip perpendicularly in his hand, like a scepter, and as his horse jogged on, the motion of his arms was not unlike the flapping of a pair of wings. A small wool hat rested on the top of his nose, for so his scanty strip of forehead might be called, and the skirts of his red coat fluttered out almost to the horse's tail. Such was the appearance of Ichabod and his steed as they shambled out of the gate of

Hans Van Ripper, and it was altogether such an apparition as is seldom to be met with in broad daylight.

It was toward evening that Ichabod arrived at the castle of the Heer Van Tassel, which he found thronged with the pride and flower of the adjacent country. Old farmers, a spare leathern-faced race, in homespun coats and breeches, blue stockings, huge shoes, and magnificent pewter buckles. Their brisk, withered little dames, in close-crimped caps, long-waisted short gowns, homespun petticoats, with scissors and pincushions, and gay calico pockets hanging on the outside. Buxom lasses, almost as antiquated as their mothers, excepting where a straw hat, a fine ribbon, or perhaps a white frock, gave symptoms of city innovation. The sons, in short square-skirted coats, with rows of stupendous brass buttons, and their hair generally queued in the fashion of the times, especially if they could procure an eel-skin for the purpose, it being esteemed throughout the country as a potent nourisher and strengthener of the hair.

Brom Bones, however, was the hero of the scene, having come to the gathering on his favorite steed, Daredevil—a creature, like himself, full of mettle and mischief, and which no one but himself could manage. He was, in fact, noted for preferring vicious animals, given to all kinds of tricks which kept the rider in constant risk of his neck, for he held a tractable, well-broken horse as unworthy of a lad of spirit.

Fain would I pause to dwell upon the world of charms that burst upon the enraptured gaze of my hero, as he entered the state parlor of Van Tassel's mansion. Not those of the bevy of buxom lasses, but the ample charms of a genuine Dutch country tea table, in the sumptuous time of autumn. Such heaped-up platters of cakes of various and almost indescribable kinds, known only to experienced Dutch housewives! There was the doughty doughnut, the tender olykoek, and the crisp and crumbling cruller; sweet cakes and short cakes, ginger cakes and honey cakes, and the whole family of cakes. And then there were apple pies, and peach pies, and pumpkin pies; besides slices of ham and smoked beef; and moreover delectable dishes of preserved plums, and peaches, and pears, and quinces; not to mention broiled shad and roasted chickens; together with bowls of milk and cream, all mingled higgledy-piggledy, pretty much as I have enumerated them, with the motherly teapot sending up its clouds of vapor from the midst—Heaven bless the mark! I want breath and time to discuss this banquet as it deserves, and am too eager to get on with my story. Happily, Ichabod Crane was not in so great a hurry as his historian, but did ample justice to every dainty.

He was a kind and thankful creature, whose heart dilated in proportion as his skin was filled with good cheer, and whose spirits rose with eating, as some men's do with drink. He could not help, too, rolling his large eyes round him as he ate, and chuckling with the possibility that he might one day be lord of all this scene of almost unimaginable luxury and splendor. Then, he thought, how soon he'd turn his back upon the old schoolhouse; snap his fingers in the face of Hans Van Ripper, and every other niggardly patron, and kick any itinerant pedagogue out of doors that should dare to call him comrade!

And now the sound of the music from the common room, or hall, summoned to the dance. Ichabod prided himself upon his dancing as much as upon his vocal powers. Not a limb, not a fiber about him was idle; and to have seen his loosely hung frame in full motion, and clattering about the room, you would have thought St. Vitus himself, that blessed patron of the dance, was figuring before you in person. The lady of his heart was his partner in the dance, and smiling graciously in reply to all his amorous oglings; while Brom Bones, sorely smitten with love and jealousy, sat brooding by himself in one corner.

But all the preceding were nothing to the tales of ghosts and apparitions that succeeded the dancing. The prevalence of supernatural stories in these parts was doubtless owing to the vicinity of Sleepy Hollow. There was a contagion in the very air that blew from that haunted region; it breathed forth an atmosphere of dreams and fancies infecting all the land. Several of the Sleepy Hollow people were present at Van Tassel's, and, as usual, were doling out their wild and wonderful legends. Many dismal tales were told about funeral trains, and mourning cries and wailings heard and seen about the great tree where the unfortunate Major André was taken, and which stood in the neighborhood. Some mention was made also of the woman in white that haunted the dark glen at Raven Rock, and was often heard to shriek on winter nights before a storm, having perished there in the snow. The chief part of the stories, however, turned upon the favorite specter of Sleepy Hollow, the Headless Horseman, who had been heard several times of late, patrolling the country; and, it was said, tethered his horse nightly among the graves in the churchyard.

The tale was told of old Brouwer, a most heretical disbeliever in ghosts, how he met the Horseman returning from his foray into Sleepy Hollow, and was obliged to get up behind him; how they galloped over bush and brake, over hill and swamp, until they reached the bridge; when the Horseman suddenly turned into a skeleton, threw old Brouwer into the brook, and sprang away over the tree-tops with a clap of thunder.

This story was immediately matched by a thrice marvellous adventure of Brom Bones, who made light of the Galloping Hessian as an arrant jockey. He affirmed that on returning one night from the neighboring village of Sing Sing, he had been overtaken by this midnight trooper; that he had offered to race with him for a bowl of punch, and should have won it too, for Daredevil beat the goblin horse all hollow, but just as they came to the church bridge, the Hessian bolted, and vanished in a flash of fire. All these tales, told in that drowsy undertone with which men talk in the dark, the countenances of the listeners only now and then receiving a casual gleam from the glare of a pipe, sank deep in the mind of Ichabod.

The revel now gradually broke up. The old farmers gathered together their families in their wagons, and were heard for some time rattling along the hollow roads, and over the distant hills. Some of the damsels mounted on pillions behind their favorite swains, and their light-hearted laughter, mingling with the clatter of hoofs, echoed along the silent woodlands, sounding fainter and fainter, until they gradually died away,—and the late scene of noise and frolic was all silent and deserted. Ichabod only lingered behind, according to the custom of country lovers, to have a tête-à-tête with the heiress; fully convinced that he was now on the high road to success. What passed at this interview I will not pretend to say, for in fact I do not know. Something, however, I fear me, must have gone wrong, for he certainly sallied forth, after no very great interval, with an air quite desolate and chapfallen. Oh, these women! these women! Could that girl have been playing off any of her coquettish tricks? Was her encouragement of the poor pedagogue all a mere sham to secure her conquest of his rival? Heaven only knows, not I! Let it suffice to say, Ichabod stole forth with the air of one who had been sacking a henhouse, rather than a fair lady's heart. Without looking to the right or left to notice the scene of rural wealth, on which he had so often gloated, he went straight to the stable, and with several hearty cuffs and kicks roused his steed most uncourteously from the comfortable quarters in which he was soundly sleeping, dreaming of mountains of corn and oats, and whole valleys of timothy and clover.

It was the very witching time of night that Ichabod, heavyhearted and crestfallen, pursued his travels homeward, along the sides of the lofty hills which rise above Tarry Town, and which he had traversed so cheerily in the afternoon. The hour was as dismal as himself. Far below him the Tappan Zee spread its dusky and indistinct waste of waters, with here and there the tall mast of a sloop, riding quietly at anchor under the land. In the dead hush of midnight, he could even hear the barking of the watchdog from the opposite shore of the Hudson; but it was so vague and faint as only to give an idea of his distance from this faithful companion of man. Now and then, too, the long-drawn crowing of a cock, accidentally awakened, would sound far, far off, from some farmhouse away among the hills—but it was like a dreaming sound in his ear. No signs of life occurred near him, but occasionally the melancholy chirp of a cricket, or perhaps the guttural twang of a bullfrog from a neighboring marsh, as if sleeping uncomfortably and turning suddenly in his bed.

All the stories of ghosts and goblins that he had heard in the afternoon now came crowding upon his recollection. The night grew darker and darker; the stars seemed to sink deeper in the sky, and driving clouds occasionally hid them from his sight. He had never felt so lonely and dismal. He was, moreover, approaching the very place where many of the scenes of the ghost stories had been laid. In the center of the road stood an enormous tulip-tree, which towered like a giant above all the other trees of the neighborhood, and formed a kind of landmark. Its limbs were gnarled and fantastic, large enough to form trunks for ordinary trees, twisting down almost to the earth, and rising again into the air. It was connected with the tragic story of the unfortunate André, who had been taken prisoner hard by; and was universally known by the name of Major André's tree. The common people regarded it with a mixture of respect and superstition, partly out of sympathy for the fate of its ill-starred namesake, and partly from the tales of strange sights, and doleful lamentations, told concerning it.

As Ichabod approached this fearful tree, he began to whistle; he thought his whistle was answered; it was but a blast sweeping sharply through the dry branches. As he approached a little nearer, he thought he saw something white, hanging in the midst of the tree: he paused and ceased whistling but, on looking more narrowly, perceived that it was a place where the tree had been scathed by lightning, and the white wood laid bare. Suddenly he heard a groan—his teeth chattered, and his knees smote against the saddle: it was but the rubbing of one huge bough upon another, as they were swayed about by the breeze. He passed the tree in safety, but new perils lay before him.

About two hundred yards from the tree, a small brook crossed the road, and ran into a marshy and thickly wooded glen, known by the name of Wiley's Swamp. A few rough logs, laid side by side, served for a bridge over this stream. On that side of the road where the brook entered the wood, a group of oaks and chestnuts, matted thick with wild grapevines, threw a cavernous gloom over it. To pass this bridge was the severest trial. It was at this identical spot that the unfortunate André was captured, and under the covert of those chestnuts and vines were the sturdy yeomen concealed who surprised him. This has ever since been considered a haunted stream, and fearful are the feelings of the schoolboy who has to pass it alone after dark.

As he approached the stream, his heart began to thump; he summoned up, however, all his resolution, gave his horse half a score of kicks in the ribs, and attempted to dash briskly across the bridge; but instead of starting forward, the perverse old animal made a lateral movement, and ran broadside against the fence. Ichabod, whose fears increased with the delay, jerked the reins on the other side, and kicked lustily with the contrary foot: it was all in vain; his steed started, it is true, but it was only to plunge to the opposite side of the road into a thicket of brambles and alder bushes. The schoolmaster now bestowed both whip and heel upon the starveling ribs of old Gunpowder, who dashed forward, snuffling and snorting, but came to a stand just by the bridge, with a suddenness that nearly sent his rider sprawling over his head. Just at this moment a splashy tramp by the side of the bridge caught the sensitive ear of Ichabod. In the dark shadow of the grove, on the margin of the brook, he beheld something huge, misshapen and towering. It stirred not, but seemed gathered up in the gloom, like some gigantic monster ready to spring upon the traveler.

The hair of the affrighted pedagogue rose upon his head with terror. What was to be done? To turn and fly was now too late; and besides, what chance was there of escaping ghost or goblin, if such it was, which could ride upon the wings of the wind? Summoning up, therefore, a show of courage, he demanded in stammering accents, "Who are you?" He received no reply. He repeated his demand in a still more agitated voice. Still there was no answer. Once more he cudgeled the sides of the inflexible Gunpowder, and, shutting his eyes, broke forth with involuntary fervor into a psalm tune. Just then the shadowy object of alarm put itself in motion, and with a scramble and a bound stood at once in the middle of the road. Though the night was dark and dismal, yet the form of the unknown might now in some degree be ascertained. He appeared to be a horseman of large dimensions, and mounted on a black horse of powerful frame. He made no offer of molestation or sociability, but kept aloof on one side of the road, jogging along on the blind side of old Gunpowder, who had now got over his fright and waywardness.

Ichabod, who had no relish for this strange midnight companion, now quickened his steed in hopes of leaving him behind. The stranger, however, quickened his horse to an equal pace. Ichabod pulled up, and fell into a walk, thinking to lag behind,—the other did the same. His heart began to sink within him; he endeavored to resume his psalm tune, but his parched tongue clove to the roof of his mouth, and he could not utter a stave. There was something in the moody and dogged silence of this pertinacious companion that was mysterious and appalling. It was soon fearfully accounted for. On mounting a rising ground, which brought the figure of his fellow-traveler in relief against the sky, gigantic in height, and muffled in a cloak, Ichabod was horror-struck on perceiving that he was headless!—but his horror was still more increased on observing that the head, which should have rested on his shoulders, was carried before him on the pommel of his saddle! His terror rose to desperation; he rained a shower of kicks and blows upon Gunpowder, hoping by a sudden movement to give his companion the slip; but the specter started full jump with him. Away, then, they dashed through thick and thin; stones flying and sparks flashing at every bound. Ichabod's flimsy garments fluttered in the air, as he stretched his long lank body away over his horse's head, in the eagerness of his flight.

They had now reached the road which turns off to Sleepy Hollow; but Gunpowder, who seemed possessed with a demon, instead of keeping up it, made an opposite turn, and plunged headlong downhill to the left. This road leads through a sandy hollow shaded by trees for about a quarter of a mile, where it crosses the bridge famous in goblin story; and just beyond swells the green knoll on which stands the whitewashed church.

As yet the panic of the steed had given his unskillful rider an apparent advantage in the chase, but just as he had got halfway through the hollow, the girths of the saddle gave way, and he felt it slipping from under him. He seized it by the pommel, and endeavored to hold it firm, but in vain; and had just time to save himself by clasping old Gunpowder round the neck, when the saddle fell to the earth, and he heard it trampled underfoot by his pursuer. For a moment the terror of Hans Van Ripper's wrath passed across his mind,—for it

was his Sunday saddle; but this was no time for petty fears; the goblin was hard on his haunches; and (unskillful rider that he was!) he had much ado to maintain his seat; sometimes slipping on one side, sometimes on another, and sometimes jolted on the high ridge of his horse's backbone, with a violence that he verily feared would cleave him asunder.

An opening in the trees now cheered him with the hopes that the church bridge was at hand. The wavering reflection of a silver star in the bosom of the brook told him that he was not mistaken. He saw the walls of the church dimly glaring under the trees beyond. "If I can but reach that bridge," thought Ichabod, "I am safe." Just then he heard the black steed panting and blowing close behind him; he even fancied that he felt his hot breath. Another convulsive kick in the ribs, and old Gunpowder sprang upon the bridge; he thundered over the resounding planks; he gained the opposite side; and now Ichabod cast a look behind to see if his pursuer should vanish, according to rule, in a flash of fire and brimstone. Just then he saw the goblin rising in his stirrups, and in the very act of hurling his head at him. Ichabod endeavored to dodge the horrible missile, but too late. It encountered his cranium with a tremendous crash,—he was tumbled headlong into the dust, and Gunpowder, the black steed, and the goblin rider passed by like a whirlwind.

The next morning the old horse was found without his saddle, and with the bridle under his feet, soberly cropping the grass at his master's gate. Ichabod did not make his appearance at breakfast; dinner-hour came, but no Ichabod. The boys assembled at the schoolhouse, and strolled idly about the banks of the brook; but no schoolmaster. Hans Van Ripper now began to feel some uneasiness about the fate of poor Ichabod, and his saddle. An inquiry was set on foot, and after diligent investigation they came upon his traces. In one part of the road leading to the church was found the saddle trampled in the dirt; the tracks of horses' hoofs deeply dented in the road, and evidently at furious speed, were traced to the bridge, beyond which, on the bank of a broad part of the brook, where the water ran deep and black, was found the hat of the unfortunate Ichabod, and close beside it a shattered pumpkin.

The brook was searched, but the body of the schoolmaster was not to be discovered. Hans Van Ripper, as executor of his estate, examined the bundle which contained all his worldly effects. They consisted of two shirts and a half; two stocks for the neck; a pair or two of worsted stockings; an old pair of corduroy smallclothes; a rusty razor; a book of psalm tunes full of dog's-ears; and a broken pitch-pipe. As to the books and furniture of the schoolhouse, they belonged to the community, excepting Cotton Mather's *History of Witchcraft*, *a New England Almanac*, and a book of dreams and fortune-telling; in which last was a sheet of foolscap much scribbled and blotted in several fruitless attempts to make a copy of verses in honor of the heiress of Van Tassel. These magic books and the poetic scrawl were forthwith consigned to the flames by Hans Van Ripper; who, from that time forward, determined to send his children no more to school, observing that he never knew any good come of this same reading and writing. Whatever money the schoolmaster possessed, and he had received his quarter's pay but a day or two before, he must have had about his person at the time of his disappearance.

The mysterious event caused much speculation at the church on the following Sunday. Knots of gazers and gossips were collected in the churchyard, at the bridge, and at the spot where the hat and pumpkin had been found. The stories of Brouwer, of Bones, and a whole array of others were called to mind; and when they had diligently considered them all, and compared them with the symptoms of the present case, they shook their heads, and came to the conclusion that Ichabod had been carried off by the Galloping Hessian. As he was a bachelor, and in nobody's debt, nobody troubled his head any more about him; the school was removed to a different quarter of the hollow, and another pedagogue reigned in his stead.

It is true, an old farmer, who had been down to New York on a visit several years after, and from whom this account of the ghostly adventure was received, brought home the intelligence that Ichabod Crane was still alive; that he had left the neighborhood partly through fear of the goblin and Hans Van Ripper, and partly in mortification at having been suddenly dismissed by the heiress; that he had changed his quarters to a distant part of the country; had kept school and studied law at the same time; had been admitted to the bar; turned politician; electioneered; written for the newspapers; and finally had been made a justice of the Ten Pound Court. Brom Bones, too, who, shortly after his rival's disappearance conducted the blooming Katrina in triumph to the altar, was observed to look exceedingly knowing whenever the story of Ichabod was related, and always burst into a hearty laugh at the mention of the pumpkin; which led some to suspect that he knew more about the matter than he chose to tell.

The old country wives, however, who are the best judges of these matters, maintain to this day that Ichabod was spirited away by supernatural means; and it is a favorite story often told about the neighborhood round the winter evening fire. The bridge became more than ever an object of superstitious awe; and that may be the reason why the road has been altered of late years, so as to approach the church by the border of the millpond. The schoolhouse, being deserted, soon fell to decay, and was reported to be haunted by the ghost of the unfortunate pedagogue; and the plowboy, loitering homeward of a still summer evening, has often fancied his voice at a distance, chanting a melancholy psalm tune among the tranquil solitudes of Sleepy Hollow.

Chapter 11

THE TELL~TALE HEART

ADAPTED FROM EDGAR ALLAN POE

True!—nervous—very, very dreadfully nervous I had been and am; but why would you say that I am mad? The disease had sharpened my senses—not destroyed—not dulled them. Above all was the sense of acute hearing. I heard all things in the heaven and in the earth. I heard many things in hell. How, then, am I mad? Hearken! and observe how healthily—how calmly I can tell you the whole story.

It is impossible to say how first the idea entered my brain; but once conceived, it haunted me day and night. Object there was none. Passion there was none. I loved the old man. He had never wronged me. He had never given me insult. For his gold I had no desire. I think it was his eye! Yes, it was this! One of his eyes resembled that of a vulture—a pale blue eye with a film over it. Whenever it fell upon me, my blood ran cold; and so by degrees—very gradually—I made up my mind to take the life of the old man and thus rid myself of the eye forever.

Now this is the point. You think me mad. Madmen know nothing. But you should have seen me. You should have seen how wisely I proceeded—with what caution—with what foresight—with what dissimulation I went to work! I was never kinder to the old man than during the whole week before I killed him. And every night, about midnight, I turned the latch of his door and opened it—oh, so gently! And then, when I had made an opening sufficient for my head, I put in a shuttered lantern, all closed, closed so that no light shone out, and then I thrust in my head. Oh, you would have laughed to see how cunningly I thrust it in! I moved it slowly—very, very slowly, so that I might not disturb the old man's sleep. It took me an hour to place my whole head within the opening so far that I could see him as he lay upon his bed. Ha!—would a madman have been so wise as this? And then, when my head was well in the room, I undid the lantern, cautiously—oh, so cautiously—cautiously (for the hinges creaked) I undid it just so much that a single thin ray fell upon the vulture eye. And this I did for seven long nights—every night just at midnight—but I found the eye always closed; and so it was impossible to do the work; for it was not the old man who vexed me, but his Evil Eye. And every morning, when the day broke, I went boldly into the chamber, and spoke courageously to him, calling him by name in a hearty tone, and inquiring how he had passed the night. So you see he would have been a profound old man, indeed, to suspect that every night, just at twelve, I looked in upon him while he slept.

Upon the eighth night I was more than usually cautious in opening the door. A watch's minute hand moves more quickly than did mine. Never before that night had I *felt* the extent of my own powers—of my sagacity. I could scarcely contain my feelings of triumph. To think that there I was, opening the door, little by little, and he not even to dream of my secret deeds or thoughts. I fairly chuckled at the idea; and perhaps he heard me—for he moved on the bed suddenly, as if startled. Now you may think that I drew back—but no. His room was as black as pitch with the thick darkness (for the shutters were close-fastened, through fear of robbers) and so I knew that he could not see the opening of the door and I kept pushing it on steadily, steadily.

I had my head in, and was about to open the lantern, when my thumb slipped upon the tin fastening and the old man sprang up in the bed, crying out, "Who's there?"

I kept quite still and said nothing. For a whole hour I did not move a muscle, and in the meantime I did not hear him lie down. He was still sitting up in the bed, listening—just as I have done, night after night, hearkening to the death-watches in the wall.

Presently I heard a groan of pain or grief— oh no!—it was the low stifled sound that arises from the bottom of the soul when overcharged with awe. I knew the sound well. Many a night, just at midnight, when all the world

slept, it has welled up from my own bosom, deepening, with its dreadful echo, the terrors that distracted me. I say I knew it well. I knew what the old man felt, and pitied him, although I chuckled at heart. I knew he had been lying awake ever since the first slight noise, when he had turned in the bed. His fears had been ever since growing upon him. He had been trying to fancy them causeless, but could not. He had been saying to himself, "It is nothing but the wind in the chimney—it is only a mouse crossing the floor," or, "It is merely a cricket which has made a single chirp." Yes, he had been trying to comfort himself with these suppositions; but he had found all in vain. *All in vain*; because Death, in approaching him, had stalked with his black shadow before him, and enveloped the victim. And it was the mournful influence of the unperceived shadow that caused him to feel—although he neither saw nor heard—to *feel* the presence of my head within the room.

When I had waited a long time, very patiently, without hearing him lie down, I resolved to open a little—a very, very little crevice in the lantern. So I opened it—you cannot imagine how stealthily, stealthily—until, at length, a single ray, like the thread of a spider, shot from out the crevice and fell upon the vulture eye.

It was open—wide, wide open—and I grew furious as I gazed upon it. I saw it with perfect distinctness—all a dull blue, with a hideous veil over it that chilled the very marrow in my bones; but I could see nothing else of the man's face or person, for I had directed the ray, as if by instinct, precisely upon the damned spot.

And now have I not told you that what you mistake for madness is but over-acuteness of the senses?—now, I say, there came to my ears a low, dull, quick sound, such as a watch makes when enveloped in cotton. I knew *that* sound well, too. It was the beating of the old man's heart. It increased my fury, as the beating of a drum stimulates the soldier into courage.

But even yet I refrained and kept still. I scarcely breathed. I held the lantern motionless. I tried to see how steadily I could maintain the ray upon the eye. Meantime the hellish beating of the heart increased. It grew quicker and quicker, and louder and louder every instant. The old man's terror *must* have been extreme! It grew louder, I say, louder every moment!—do you mark me well? I have told you I am nervous: so I am. And now, at the dead hour of the night, amid the dreadful silence of that old house, so strange a noise as this excited me to uncontrollable terror. Yet, for some minutes longer, I refrained and stood still. But the beating grew louder, louder! I thought the heart would be heard by a neighbor! The old man's hour had come! With a loud yell I threw open the lantern and leaped into the room. He shrieked once—once only. In an instant I dragged him to the floor, and pulled the heavy bed over him. I then smiled gaily, to find the deed so easily done. But, for many minutes, the heart beat on with a muffled sound. This, however, did not vex me; it would not be heard through the wall. At length it ceased. The old man was dead. I removed the bed and examined the corpse. Yes, he was stone dead. I placed my hand upon the heart and held it there many minutes. There was no pulsation. He was stone dead. His eye would trouble me no more.

If you still think me mad, you will think so no longer when I describe the wise precautions I took for the concealment of the body. The night waned,

things. But, ere long, I felt myself getting pale and wished them gone. My head ached, and I fancied a ringing in my ears; but still they sat and chatted. The ringing became more distinct—it continued and became more distinct. I talked more freely to get rid of the feeling; but it continued and gained definitiveness—until, at length, I found that the noise was *not* within my ears.

No doubt I now grew very pale; but I talked more fluently, and with a heightened voice. Yet the sound increased—and what could I do? It was *a low, dull, quick sound—much such a sound as a watch makes when it is enveloped in cotton.* I gasped for breath—and yet the officers heard it not. I talked more quickly—more vehemently; but the noise steadily increased. I arose and argued about trifles, in a high key and with violent gesticulations; but the noise steadily increased. Why *would* they not be gone? I paced the floor to and fro with heavy strides, as if excited to fury by the observations of the men—but the noise steadily increased. O God! what could I do? I foamed—I raved—I swore! I swung the chair upon which I had been sitting, and grated it upon the floorboards, but the noise arose over all and increased. It grew louder—louder—*louder*! And still the men chatted pleasantly and smiled. Was it possible they heard not? Almighty God!—no, no! They heard!—they suspected! they *knew*!—they were making a mockery of my horror!—this I thought and this I think. But anything was better than this agony! Anything was more tolerable than this derision! I could bear those hypocritical smiles no longer! I felt that I must scream or die!—and now—again! hark! louder! louder! louder! *louder!*

"Villains!" I shrieked. "Dissemble no more! I admit the deed!—tear up the planks!—here, here!—it is the beating of his hideous heart!"

Chapter III

THE MUMMY'S CURSE

ADAPTED FROM LOUISA MAY ALCOTT

"And what are these, Paul?" asked Evelyn, opening a tarnished gold box and examining its contents curiously.

"Seeds of some unknown Egyptian plant," replied Forsyth, with a sudden shadow on his dark face, as he looked down at the scarlet grains lying in the white hand lifted to him.

"Where did you get them?" asked the girl.

"That is a weird story, which will only haunt you if I tell it," said Forsyth, with an absent expression that strongly excited the girl's curiosity.

"Please tell it—I like weird tales, and they never trouble me. Ah, do tell it; your stories are always so interesting," she cried, looking up with such a pretty blending of entreaty and command in her charming face, that refusal was impossible.

"You'll be sorry for it, and so shall I, perhaps; I warn you beforehand, that harm is foretold to the possessor of those mysterious seeds," said Forsyth, smiling, even while he knit his black brows, and regarded the blooming creature before him with a fond yet foreboding glance.

"Tell on! I'm not afraid of these pretty little things," she answered, with an imperious nod.

"To hear is to obey. Let me read the facts, and then I will begin," returned Forsyth, pacing to and fro with the far-off look of one who turns the pages of the past.

Evelyn watched him a moment, and then returned to her work, or play, rather, for the task seemed well suited to the vivacious little creature, half-child, half-woman.

"While in Egypt," commenced Forsyth, slowly, "I went one day with my guide and Professor Niles, to explore the Cheops Pyramid. Niles had a mania for antiquities of all sorts, and forgot time, danger, and fatigue in the ardor of his pursuit. We rummaged up and down the narrow passages, half choked with dust and close air; reading inscriptions on the walls, stumbling over shattered mummy-cases, or coming face-to-face with some shriveled specimen perched like a hobgoblin on the little shelves where the dead used to be stowed away for ages. I was desperately tired after a few hours of it, and begged the professor to return. But he was bent on exploring certain places, and would not desist. We had but one guide, so I was forced to stay; but Jumal, seeing how weary I was, proposed to us to rest in one of the larger passages, while he went to procure another guide for Niles. We consented, and assuring us that we were perfectly safe, if we did not quit the spot, Jumal left us, promising to return speedily. The professor sat down to take notes of his researches, and stretching myself on the soft sand, I fell asleep.

"I was roused by that indescribable chill which instinctively warns one of danger, and springing up, I found myself alone. One torch burned faintly where Jumal had struck it, but Niles and the other light were gone. A dreadful sense of loneliness oppressed me for a moment; then I collected myself and looked well about me. A bit of paper was pinned to my hat, which lay near me, and on it, in the professor's writing were these words:

"'I've gone back a little to refresh my memory on certain points. Don't follow me till Jumal comes. I can find my way back to you, for I have a clue. Sleep well, and dream gloriously of the Pharaohs. N. N.'

"I laughed at first over the old enthusiast, then felt anxious, then restless, and finally resolved to follow him, for I discovered a strong cord fastened to a fallen stone, and knew that this was the clue he spoke of. Leaving a note for Jumal, I took my torch and retraced my steps, following the cord along the winding ways. I often shouted, but received no reply, and pressed on, hoping at each turn to see the old man poring over some musty relic of antiquity. Suddenly the cord ended, and lowering my torch, I saw that the footsteps had gone on.

"'Rash fellow, he'll lose himself, to a certainty,' I thought, really alarmed now.

"As I paused, a faint call reached me, and I answered it, waited, shouted again, and a still fainter echo replied.

"Niles was evidently going on, misled by the reverberations of the low passages. No time was to be lost, and, forgetting myself, I stuck my torch in the deep sand to guide me back to the clue, and ran down the straight path before me, whooping like a madman as I went. I did not mean to lose sight of the light, but in my eagerness to find Niles I turned from the main passage, and, guided by his voice, hastened on. His torch soon gladdened my eyes, and the clutch of his trembling hands told me what agony he had suffered.

"'Let us get out of this horrible place at once,' he said, wiping great drops off his forehead.

"'Come, we're not far from the clue. I can soon reach it, and then we are safe'; but as I spoke, a chill passed over me, for a perfect labyrinth of narrow paths lay before us.

"Trying to guide myself by such land-marks as I had observed in my hasty passage, I followed the tracks in the sand till I fancied we must be near my light. No glimmer appeared, however, and kneeling down to examine the foot-prints nearer, I discovered, to my dismay, that I had been following the wrong ones, for among those marked by a deep boot heel, were prints of bare feet; we had had no guide there, and Jumal wore sandals.

"Rising, I confronted Niles, with the one despairing word, 'Lost!' as I pointed from the treacherous sand to the fast-waning light.

"I thought the old man would be overwhelmed but, to my surprise, he grew quite calm and steady, thought a moment, and then went on, saying, quietly:

"'Other men have passed here before us; let us follow their steps, for, if I do not greatly err, they lead toward larger passages, where one's way is easily found.'

"On we went, bravely, till a misstep threw the professor violently to the ground with a broken leg, and nearly extinguished the torch. It was a horrible predicament, and I gave up all hope as I sat beside the poor fellow, who lay exhausted with fatigue, remorse, and pain, for I would not leave him.

"'Paul,' he said suddenly, 'if you will not go on, there is one more effort we can make. I remember hearing that a party, lost as we are, saved themselves by building a fire. The smoke penetrated further than sound or light, and the guide's quick wit understood the unusual mist; he followed it, and rescued the party. Make a fire and trust to Jumal.'

"'A fire without wood?' I began; but he pointed to a shelf behind me, which had escaped me in the gloom; and on it I saw a slender mummy case. I understood him, for these dry cases, which lie about in hundreds, are freely used as firewood. Reaching up, I pulled it down, believing it to be empty, but as it fell, it burst open, and out rolled a mummy. Accustomed as I was to such sights, it startled me a little, for danger had unstrung my nerves. Laying the little brown cocoon aside, I smashed the case, lit the pile with my torch, and soon a light cloud of smoke drifted down the three passages which diverged from the cell-like place where we had paused.

"While busied with the fire, Niles, forgetful of pain and peril, had dragged the mummy nearer, and was examining it with the interest of a man whose ruling passion was strong even in death.

"'Come and help me unroll this. I have always longed to be the first to see the curious treasures put away among the folds of these uncanny winding-sheets. This is a woman, and we may find something rare and precious here,' he said, beginning to unfold the outer coverings, from which a strange aromatic odor came.

"Reluctantly I obeyed, for to me there was something sacred in the bones

of this unknown woman. But to pass the time and amuse the poor fellow, I lent a hand, wondering as I worked, if this dark, ugly thing had ever been a lovely, soft-eyed Egyptian girl.

"From the fibrous folds of the wrappings dropped precious gums and spices, which half intoxicated us with their potent breath, antique coins, and a curious jewel or two, which Niles eagerly examined.

"All the bandages but one were cut off at last, and a small head laid bare, round which still hung great plaits of what had once been luxuriant hair. The shriveled hands were folded on the breast, and clasped in them lay that gold box."

"Oh!" cried Evelyn, dropping it from her rosy palm with a shudder.

"Nay; don't reject the poor little mummy's treasure. I never have quite forgiven myself for stealing it, or for burning her," said Forsyth, breathing heavily, as the recollection of that experience sent his pulse racing.

"Burning her! Oh, Paul, what do you mean?" asked the girl, sitting up with a face full of excitement.

"I'll tell you. While busied with Madam Mummy, our fire had burned low, for the dry case went like tinder. A faint, far-off sound made our hearts leap, and Niles cried out: 'Pile on the wood; Jumal is tracking us; don't let the smoke fail now or we are lost!'

"'There is no more wood; the case was very small, and is all gone,' I answered, tearing off such of my garments as would burn readily, and piling them upon the embers.

"Niles did the same, but the light fabrics were quickly consumed, and made no smoke.

"'Burn that!' commanded the professor, pointing to the mummy.

"I hesitated a moment. Again came the faint echo of a horn. Life was dear to me. A few dry bones might save us, and I obeyed him in silence.

"A dull blaze sprang up, and a heavy smoke rose from the burning mummy, rolling in volumes through the low passages, and threatening to suffocate us with its fragrant mist. My brain grew dizzy, the light danced before my eyes, strange phantoms seemed to people the air, and, in the act of asking Niles why he gasped and looked so pale, I lost consciousness."

Evelyn drew a long breath, and removed the scented box and its contents from her lap as if its odor oppressed her.

Forsyth's swarthy face was all aglow with the excitement of his story, and his black eyes glittered as he added, with a quick laugh:

"That's all; Jumal found and got us out, and we both forswore pyramids for the rest of our days."

"But the box: how came you to keep it?" asked Evelyn, eyeing it askance as it lay gleaming in a streak of sunshine.

"Oh, I brought it away as a souvenir, and Niles kept the other trinkets."

"But you said harm was foretold to the possessor of those scarlet seeds," persisted the girl, whose fancy was excited by the tale, and who fancied all was not told.

"Among his spoils, Niles found a bit of parchment, which he deciphered, and this inscription said that the mummy we had so ungallantly burned was that of a famous sorceress who bequeathed her curse to whoever should disturb her rest. Of course I don't believe that curse has anything to do with it, but it's a fact that Niles never prospered from that day. He says it's because he has never recovered from the fall and fright and I daresay it is so; but I sometimes wonder if I am to share the curse, for I've a vein of superstition in me, and that poor little mummy haunts my dreams still."

A long silence followed these words. Paul stared into the distance, and Evelyn lay regarding him with a thoughtful face. But gloomy fancies were as foreign to her nature as shadows are to noonday, and presently she laughed a cheery laugh, saying as she took up the box again:

"Why don't you plant them, and see what wondrous flower they will bear?"

"I doubt if they would bear anything after lying in a mummy's hand for centuries," replied Forsyth, gravely.

"Let me plant them and try. You know wheat has sprouted and grown that was taken from a mummy's coffin; why should not these pretty seeds? I should so like to watch them grow; may I, Paul?"

"No, I'd rather leave that experiment untried. I have a queer feeling about the matter, and don't want to meddle myself or let anyone I love meddle with these seeds. They may be some horrible poison, or possess some evil power, for the sorceress evidently valued them, since she clutched them fast even in her tomb."

"Now, you are foolishly superstitious, and I laugh at you. Be generous; give me one seed, just to learn if it will grow. See, I'll pay for it," and Evelyn, who now stood beside him, dropping a kiss on his forehead as she made her request, with the most engaging air.

But Forsyth would not yield. He smiled and returned the embrace with lov-erlike warmth, then flung the seeds into the fire, and gave her back the golden box, saying, tenderly:

"My darling, I'll fill it with diamonds or bonbons, if you please, but I will not let you play with that witch's spells. You've enough of your own, so for-get the 'pretty seeds' and see what an enchantress you've become to me."

Evelyn frowned, and smiled, and presently the lovers were out in the spring sunshine reveling in their own happy hopes, untroubled by one fore-boding fear.

"I have a little surprise for you, love," said Forsyth, as he greeted his fiancée three months later on the morning of their wedding day.

"And I have one for you," she answered, smiling faintly.

"How pale you are, and how thin you grow! All this bridal bustle is too much for you, Evelyn," he said, with fond anxiety, as he watched the strange pallor of her face, and pressed the wasted little hand in his.

"I am so tired," she said, and leaned her head wearily on her lover's breast. "Neither sleep, food, nor air gives me strength, and a curious mist seems to cloud my mind at times. Mamma says it is the heat, but I shiver even in the sun, while at night I burn with fever. Paul, dear, I'm glad you are going to take me away to lead a quiet, happy life with you, but I'm afraid it will be a very short one."

"My fanciful little wife! You are tired and nervous with all this worry, but a few weeks of rest in the country will give me back my blooming Eve again. Have you no curiosity to learn my surprise?" he asked, to change her thoughts.

The vacant look stealing over the girl's face gave place to one of interest, but as she listened it seemed to require an effort to fix her mind on her lover's words.

"You remember the day we opened that old gold box?"

"Yes," and a smile touched her lips for a moment.

"And how you wanted to plant those queer red seeds I stole from the mummy?"

"I remember," and her eyes kindled with sudden fire.

"Well, I tossed them into the fire, as I thought, and gave you the box. But when I went back, and found one of those seeds on the rug, a sudden fancy to gratify your whim led me to send it to Niles and ask him to plant it and report on its progress. Today I hear from him for the first time, and he reports that the seed has grown marvelously, has budded, and that he intends to take the first flower, if it blooms in time, to a meeting of agricultural experts, after which he will send me its true name and the plant itself. From his description, it must be very curious, and I'm impatient to see it."

"You need not wait; I can show you the flower in its bloom," and Evelyn beckoned with the beguiling smile so long a stranger to her lips.

Much amazed, Forsyth followed her to her little boudoir, and there, standing in the sunshine, was the unknown plant. Almost rank in their lux-uriance were the vivid green leaves on the slender purple stems, and rising from the midst, one ghostly white flower, shaped like the head of a hooded snake, with scarlet stamens like forked tongues; and on the petals glittered spots like dew.

"A strange, uncanny flower! Has it any odor?" asked Forsyth, bending to examine it, and forgetting, in his interest, to ask how it came there.

"None, and that disappoints me; I am so fond of perfumes," answered the girl, caressing the green leaves which trembled at her touch, while the purple stems deepened their tint.

"Now tell me about it," said Forsyth, after standing silent for several minutes.

"I, too, found a seed that had fallen on the rug. I planted it under a glass in the richest soil I could find, watered it faithfully, and was amazed at the rapidity with which it grew when once it appeared above the earth. I told no one, for I meant to surprise you with it; but this bud has been so long in blooming, I have had to wait. It is a good omen that it blossoms today, and as it is nearly white, I mean to wear it, for I've learned to love it, having been my pet for so long."

"I would not wear it," cautioned Forsyth, "for in spite of its innocent color, it is an evil-looking plant, with its adder's tongue and unnatural dew. Wait till Niles tells us what it is, then pet it if it is harmless. Perhaps the sorceress cherished it for some symbolic beauty—those old Egyptians were full of fancies. It was very sly of you to turn the tables on me in this way. But I forgive you, since in a few hours, I shall claim your enchanted hand forever. How cold it is! Come out into the garden and get some warmth and color for tonight, my love."

But when night came, no one could reproach the girl with her pallor, for she glowed like a pomegranate flower, her eyes were full of fire, her lips scarlet, and all her old vivacity seemed to have returned. A more brilliant bride never blushed under a misty veil, and when her lover saw her, he was absolutely startled by the almost unearthly beauty which transformed the pale, languid creature of the morning into this radiant woman.

They were married, and if love, many blessings, and all good gifts lavishly showered upon them could make them happy, then this young pair were truly blessed. But even in the rapture of the moment that made her his, Forsyth observed how icy cold was the little hand he held, how feverish the deep color on the soft cheek he kissed, and what a strange fire burned in the tender eyes that looked so wistfully at him.

Blithe and beautiful as a spirit, the smiling bride played her part in all the festivities of that long evening, and when at last light, life and color began to fade, the loving eyes that watched her thought it but the natural weariness of the hour. As the last guest departed, Forsyth was met by a servant, who gave him a letter marked "Urgent." Tearing it open, he read these lines, from a friend of the professor's:

Dear Sir—

Poor Niles died suddenly two days ago, while at the Scientific Club, and his last words were: "Tell Paul Forsyth to beware of the Mummy's Curse, for this fatal flower has killed me." The circumstances of his death were so peculiar, that I add them as a sequel to this message. For several months, as he told us, he had been watching an unknown plant, and that evening he brought us the flower to examine. Other matters of interest absorbed us till a late hour, and the plant was forgotten. The professor wore it in his buttonhole—a strange white, serpent-headed blossom, with pale glittering spots, which slowly changed to a glittering scarlet, till the leaves looked as if sprinkled with blood. It was observed that instead of the pallor and feebleness which had recently come over him, that the professor was unusually animated, and seemed in an almost unnatural state of high spirits. Near the close of the meeting, in the midst of a lively discussion, he suddenly dropped, as if smitten with apoplexy. He was conveyed home insensible, and after one lucid interval, in which he gave me the message I have recorded above, he died in great agony, raving of mummies, pyramids, serpents, and some fatal curse which had fallen upon him.

After his death, livid scarlet spots, like those on the flower, appeared upon his skin, and he shriveled like a withered leaf. At my desire, the mysterious plant was examined, and pronounced by the best authority one of the most deadly poisons known to the Egyptian sorceresses. The plant slowly absorbs the vitality of whoever cultivates it, and the blossom, worn for two or three hours, produces either madness or death.

Down dropped the paper from Forsyth's hand; he read no further, but hurried back into the room where he had left his young wife. As if worn out with fatigue, she had thrown herself upon a couch, and lay there motionless.

"Evelyn, my dearest! Wake up and answer me. Did you wear that strange flower today?" whispered Forsyth.

There was no need for her to answer, for there, gleaming spectrally on her bosom, was the evil blossom, its white petals spotted now with flecks of scarlet, vivid as drops of newly spilt blood.

But the unhappy bridegroom scarcely saw it, for the face above it appalled him by its utter vacancy. Drawn and pallid, as if with some wasting malady, the young face, so lovely an hour ago, lay before him aged and blighted by the baleful influence of the plant which had drunk up her life. No recognition in the eyes, no word upon the lips, no motion of the hand—only the faint breath and the fluttering pulse, revealed that she was alive.

Alas for the young wife! The superstitious fear at which she had smiled had proved true: the curse that had bided its time for ages was fulfilled at last, and her own hand wrecked her happiness forever. Death in life was her doom, and for years Forsyth secluded himself to tend with pathetic devotion the pale ghost, who never, by word or look, could thank him for the love that outlived even such a fate as this.

chapter iv

THE CANTERVILLE GHOST

ADAPTED FROM OSCAR WILDE

When Mr. Hiram B. Otis, of the American consulate, bought Canterville Chase, everyone told him he was doing a very foolish thing, as there was no doubt at all that the place was haunted. Canterville himself, who was a man of the most punctilious honor, had felt it his duty to mention the fact to Mr. Otis when they came to discuss terms.

"We have not cared to live in the place ourselves," said Lord Canterville, "since my great-aunt, the Dowager Duchess of Bolton, was frightened into a fit, from which she never really recovered, by two skeleton hands being placed on her shoulders as she was dressing for dinner, and I feel bound to tell you, Mr. Otis, that the Ghost has been seen by several living members of my family as well as the rector of the parish. After the unfortunate accident to the duchess, none of the younger servants would stay with us, in consequence of the mysterious noises that came from the corridor and the Library."

"My Lord," answered the Consul, "I will take the furniture and the Ghost as a package deal. I admire the craftsmanship of the former and very much doubt the existence of the latter."

"I fear the Ghost exists," said Lord Canterville; "it has been well known

for three centuries, since 1584 in fact, and always makes its appearance before the death of any member of our family."

"Well, so does the family doctor for that matter, Lord Canterville. But there is no such thing, sir, as a ghost, and I guess the laws of nature are not going to be suspended for the British aristocracy."

"You Americans are certainly very pragmatic," answered Lord Canterville, "and if you don't mind a ghost in the house, then so be it. Only you must remember I warned you."

A few weeks after this, the purchase was completed, and the Consul and his family moved into Canterville Chase. Mrs. Otis, who had been a celebrated New York belle, was now an attractive, middle-aged woman with fine eyes and a superb profile. She had a magnificent constitution and a really wonderful amount of animal spirits. Her eldest son, Washington, was a fair-haired, rather good-looking young man who was well known on both sides of the Atlantic for being an excellent dancer. Miss Virginia E. Otis was a little girl of fifteen, lithe and lovely as a fawn and with a fine freedom in her large blue eyes. She was a great horsewoman and was often seen galloping around the estate on her pony. After Virginia came the twins, who were really delightful boys, though with a tendency to cause a considerable amount of mischief.

As Canterville Chase is seven miles from the nearest railway station, Mr. Otis had telegraphed ahead for a carriage to meet them, and they started on their drive in high spirits. It was a lovely July evening, and the air was delicate with the scent of the pine woods. Little squirrels peered at them from behind the beech trees as they went by, and rabbits scampered away through the brush and over the mossy knolls, with their white tails in the air. As they entered the avenue of Canterville Chase, however, the sky became suddenly overcast with clouds, and a curious stillness seemed to hold the atmosphere; a great flight of crows passed silently over their heads and, before they reached the house, some big drops of rain had fallen.

Mrs. Umley, the old housekeeper, was there to greet them, making each a low curtsey as they alighted from the carriage, saying in a quaint, old-fashioned manner, "I bid you welcome to Canterville Chase." Following her, they passed through the fine Tudor hall into the Library, a long, low room, paneled in black oak, at the end of which there was a large stained-glass window. Here they found a meal had been laid for them, and after taking off their wraps, they sat and began to look round, while Mrs. Umley waited on them.

Suddenly Mrs. Otis caught sight of a dull red stain on the floor by the fireplace and, quite unconscious of what it signified, said to Mrs. Umley, "I'm afraid something has been spilt there."

"Yes, madam," replied the old housekeeper in a low voice, "blood has been spilt on that spot."

"How horrid," cried Mrs. Otis; "I don't at all care for bloodstains in a sitting room. It must be removed at once."

The old woman smiled and answered in the same low, mysterious voice, "It is the blood of Lady Eleanor de Canterville, who was murdered on that very spot by her own husband, Sir Simon de Canterville, in 1575. Sir Simon survived her but disappeared under very mysterious circumstances. His body has never been discovered, but his guilty spirit still haunts the Chase.

The bloodstain cannot be removed."

"Nonsense," cried Washington Otis; "Pinkerton's Champion Stain Remover will clean it up in no time," and before the terrified housekeeper could interfere, he had fallen upon his knees and was rapidly scouring the floor with a small stick of what looked like a black cosmetic. In a few moments no trace of the bloodstain could be seen.

"I knew Pinkerton's would do it," he exclaimed triumphantly, as he looked round at his admiring family; but no sooner had he said these words than a terrible flash of lightning lit up the somber room, a fearful clap of thunder made them all start to their feet, and Mrs. Umley fainted.

"What a monstrous climate!" said the American Consul as he calmly lit a long cigar. In a few minutes the old woman came to and, visibly upset, sternly warned Mr. Otis to beware of trouble coming to the house: "I have seen things with my own eyes, sir," she said, "that would make any Christian's hair stand on end, and many and many a night I have not closed my eyes in sleep for the awful things that are done here." Mr. Otis and his wife, however, warmly assured the honest soul that they were not afraid of ghosts, and after invoking the blessings of providence on her new master and mistress, the old housekeeper tottered off to her own room.

The storm raged fiercely all night, but nothing of particular note occurred. The next morning, however, when they came down to breakfast, they found the terrible stain of blood once again on the floor. Washington accordingly rubbed out the spot with his stick of Pinkerton's, but on the second morning it appeared again. The third morning it was also there, though the Library had been locked up at night by Mr. Otis himself and the key carried upstairs. The whole family was now quite interested, and Mr. Otis began to suspect that he had been too dogmatic in his denial of the existence of ghosts. If anyone was still skeptical, all doubts about the objective reality of phantasmata were dispelled that night.

Sometime after midnight, Mr. Otis was wakened by a curious noise in the corridor outside his room. It sounded like the clank of metal and seemed to be coming nearer every moment. He got up at once, struck a match, and looked at the time. It was exactly one o'clock. He was quite calm and felt his pulse, which was not at all feverish. The strange noise continued, and with it he heard distinctly the sound of footsteps. He put on his slippers, took a small phial out of his night table, and opened the door. Right in front of him he saw, in the wan moonlight, an old man of terrible aspect. His eyes were as red as burning coals; long gray hair fell over his shoulders in matted coils; his garments, which were of antique cut, were soiled and ragged, and from his wrists and ankles hung heavy rusted iron manacles.

"My dear sir," said Mr. Otis, "I really must insist on your oiling those chains and have brought you for that purpose a small bottle of the Tammany Rising Sun Lubricator. It is said to be completely efficacious upon one application, and there are several testimonials to that effect on the package. I shall leave it here for you by the bedroom candles and will be happy to supply you with more should you require it." With these words the United States consul laid the bottle down on the marble table and, closing his door, retired to rest.

For a moment the Canterville Ghost stood quite motionless in natural indignation; then, dashing the bottle violently on the polished floor, he fled down the corridor, uttering hollow groans and emitting a ghastly green light. Just, however, as he reached the top of the great oak staircase, a door was flung open, two little white-robed figures appeared, and a large pillow whizzed past his head! There was evidently no time to be lost, so, hastily adopting the Fourth Dimension of Space as a means of escape, he vanished through the wainscoting and the house became quiet.

On reaching a small secret chamber in the west wing, he leaned up against a moonbeam to recover his breath and began to try and realize his position. Never, in a brilliant and uninterrupted career of three hundred years, had he been so grossly insulted. He thought of the Dowager Duchess, whom he had frightened into a fit as she stood before the mirror in her lace and diamonds; of the four housemaids, who had gone off in hysterics when he merely grinned at them through the curtains of their bedroom; of old Madame de Tremouillac, who, having wakened up one morning early and seen a skeleton seated in an armchair reading her diary, had been confined to her bed for six weeks with an attack of brain fever. He remembered the terrible night when the wicked Lord Canterville was found choking in his dressing-room with the knave of diamonds halfway down his throat, and confessed, just before he died, that he had cheated Charles James Fox out of fifty thousand pounds in a game of whist by means of that very card and swore that the Ghost had made him swallow it.

All his great achievements came back to him again, from the butler that had shot himself in the pantry because he had seen a green hand tapping at the window pane, to the beautiful Lady Stutfield, who was always obliged to wear a black velvet band round her throat to hide the marks of five fingers burned upon her skin and who drowned herself at last in the carp pond at the end of King's Walk. With the enthusiasm of the true artist he went over his most celebrated performances and smiled bitterly to himself as he recalled to mind his last appearance as "Red Reuben, or the Strangled Babe," his debut as "Gaunt Gideon, the Bloodsucker of Bexley Moor," and the furor he had excited one lovely June evening by merely playing ninepins with his own bones upon the croquet lawn. And after all this, some wretched modern Americans were to come and offer the Rising Sun Lubricator and throw pillows at his head! It was quite unbearable. Besides, no ghost in history had been treated in this manner. Accordingly, he determined to have vengeance and remained till daylight in an attitude of deep thought.

A week went by before the Ghost made his second appearance. Shortly after they had all gone to bed they were suddenly alarmed by a fearful crash in the hall. Rushing downstairs, they found that a large suit of old armor had become detached from its stand and had fallen on the stone floor, while seated in a high-backed chair was the Canterville Ghost, rubbing his knees with an expression of acute agony on his face. The twins, ever prepared, loosed two pellets from their trusty pea-shooters while the Consul covered him with a revolver and called upon him, in accordance with western frontier etiquette, to put up his hands! The Ghost jumped up with a shriek of wild rage and swept through them like a mist, extinguishing Washington Otis's candle as he passed, leaving them in total darkness. On reaching the top of the staircase he recovered himself and determined to give his celebrated peal of demonic laughter. This was a sound so terrible that it was said to turn Lord Raker's hair gray in a single night and had made three of Lady Canterville's French governesses give notice before their month was up. He accordingly laughed his most horrible laugh, till the old vaulted roof rang and rang again, but hardly had the fearful echo died away when a door opened and Mrs. Otis came out in a light blue dressing gown. "I'm afraid you are far from well," she said, "so I've brought you a bottle of Dr. Dobell's patent medicine. If it is indigestion, you will find it a most excellent remedy." The Ghost glared at her in fury and prepared to turn himself into a large black dog but, upon hearing footsteps approaching, contented himself with becoming faintly phosphorescent and vanished with a deep churchyard groan, just as the twins came up to him.

A fortnight later, the Ghost resolved to make one more attempt to frighten these loathsome Americans and, accordingly, dressed himself as his celebrated character "Reckless Rupert, or the Headless Earl." When all was ready to his satisfaction, at a quarter past one he glided out of the wainscoting and crept down the corridor. On reaching the room occupied by the twins, he found the door ajar. Wishing to make an effective entrance, he flung it wide open, when a heavy jug of water fell right down on him, wetting him to the skin and just missing his left shoulder by a couple of inches. At the same moment he heard stifled shrieks of laughter coming from the four-poster bed. The shock to his nervous system was so great that he fled back to his room fast as he could go and the next day he was laid up with a severe cold. The only thing that consoled him in the whole affair was the fact that he had not brought his head with him, for, had he done so, the consequences might have been very serious.

After this debacle, the Ghost was so dispirited (as it were) that he gave up trying to frighten the Consul and his family, and as the weeks went by he was all but a forgotten presence in the Chase. One afternoon, Virginia was taking a short-cut in the mansion on her way to the stables where she kept her pony. She passed the rarely used Tapestry Chamber and, seeing the door open, looked in to see who might be there. To her immense surprise it was the Canterville Ghost himself! He was sitting by the window, watching the ruined gold of the yellowing trees fly through the air and the red leaves dancing madly down the long avenue. His head was leaning on his hand, and his whole attitude was one of deep depression. Indeed, so forlorn did he look, that little Virginia, whose first idea was to run and lock herself in her room, was filled with pity and resolved to try and comfort him.

"I am sorry for you," she said, "but my brothers are going back to school tomorrow, and if you behave yourself, no one will bother you."

"It is absurd to ask me to behave myself," he answered, looking round in astonishment at the pretty girl who had ventured to address him, "quite absurd. I must rattle my chains and groan through keyholes and walk around at night. It is my only reason for existing."

"It is no reason at all for existing, and you know you've been very wicked. Mrs. Umley told us, the first day we arrived, that you had killed your wife."

"Well, I quite admit it," said the Ghost petulantly, "but it was purely a

G̶h̶o̶s̶t̶s̶

family matter and concerned no one else."

"It is very wrong to kill anyone," said Virginia, who at times had a sweet Puritan gravity, inherited from some New England ancestor.

"Well, all that's over and done with," replied the Ghost, "and haven't I been punished enough? First starved to death by her brothers and now I'm so lonely and so unhappy that I really don't know what to do. I wish I could just go to sleep but I can't."

"That's quite absurd! You merely have to go to bed and blow out the candle. It is very difficult sometimes to stay awake, especially in church, but there is no difficulty at all about going to sleep. Why, even babies know how to do it, and they aren't very clever."

"I have not slept for three hundred years," he said sadly, and Virginia's beautiful blue eyes opened in wonder; "for three hundred years I have not slept and I am so tired."

Virginia grew quite grave and her little lips trembled like rose leaves. She came toward him and, kneeling down at his side, looked up into his weathered old face.

"Poor, poor Ghost," she murmured; "have you no place where you can sleep?"

"Far away beyond the pine woods," he answered, in a low and dreamy voice, "there is a little garden. There the grass grows long and deep, there are great white stars of the hemlock flower, there the nightingale sings all night long. All night long he sings, and the cold, crystal moon looks down, and the yew tree spreads out its giant arms over the sleepers."

Virginia's eyes grew dim with tears, and she hid her face in her hands. "You mean the Garden of Death," she whispered.

"Yes, Death. Death must be so beautiful. To lie in the soft brown earth, with grasses waving above one's head, and listen to silence. To have no yesterday and no tomorrow. To forget time, to forgive life, to be at peace. You can help me. You can open for me the portals of Death's house, for Love is always with you and Love is stronger than Death is."

Virginia trembled, a cold shudder ran through her, and for a few moments there was silence. She felt as if she were in a terrible dream.

Then the Ghost spoke again, and his voice sounded like the sighing of the wind.

"Have you ever read the old prophecy on the Library window?"

"Oh, often," cried the little girl, looking up; "I know it quite well. It is painted in curious black letters and it is difficult to read. There are only six lines:

When a golden girl can win
Prayer from out the lips of sin,
When the barren almond bears,
And a little child gives away its tears,
Then shall all the house be still
And peace come to Canterville.

But I don't know what they mean."

"They mean," he said sadly, "that you must weep for me for my sins, because

I have no tears, and pray with me for my soul, because I have no faith, and then, if you have always been sweet and good and gentle, the Angel of Death will have mercy on me. You will see fearful shapes in darkness and wicked voices will whisper in your ear, but they will not harm you, for against the purity of a little child the powers of hell cannot prevail."

Virginia made no answer, and the Ghost wrung his hands in wild despair as he looked down on her golden head. Suddenly she stood up, very pale and with a strange light in her eyes. "I am not afraid," she said firmly, "and I will ask the Angel of Death to have mercy on you."

He rose from his seat with a faint cry of joy and, taking her hand, bent over it with old-fashioned grace and kissed it. His fingers were cold as ice and his lips burned like fire, but Virginia did not falter as he led her across the dusky room. On the faded green tapestry were embroidered little huntsmen. They blew their tasseled horns and with their tiny hands waved to her to go back. "Go back! Little Virginia," they cried, "go back!" but the Ghost clutched her hand more tightly and she shut her eyes against them. Horrible animals with lizard tails and goggle eyes blinked at her from the carved chimney-piece and murmured, "Beware! Little Virginia, beware! We may never see you again," but the Ghost glided on more swiftly and Virginia did not listen. When they reached the end of the room, he stopped and muttered some words she could not understand. She opened her eyes and saw the wall slowly fading away like a mist and a great black cavern in front of her. A bitter cold wind swept round them, and she felt something pulling at her dress. "Quick, quick," cried the Ghost, "or it will be too late," and, in a moment, the wainscoting had closed behind them and the Tapestry Chamber was empty.

Three long days passed without a word or a clue as to Virginia's where-abouts, and the Otis family was in a terrible state of despair. On the evening of the third day, having resolved to telegraph Scotland Yard in the morning as a last, desperate attempt to ascertain the fate of the missing girl, the family sat down to a melancholy meal which no one, not even the twins, felt like eating. Just as they were leaving the dining room, midnight began to boom from the clock tower, and when the last stroke sounded, they heard a crash and a sud-den shrill cry; a peal of thunder shook the house, a strain of unearthly music floated through the air, a panel at the top of the staircase flew back with a loud noise, and out on the landing, looking very pale and white, stepped Virginia. In a moment they all rushed up to her. Her mother clasped her to her breast while the rest looked on in amazed bewilderment.

"Good heavens, child! Where have you been?" said Mr. Otis when he had recovered his voice.

"Papa," said Virginia quietly, "I have been with the Ghost. He is dead and you must come and see him."

Turning round, the girl led her family through the opening in the wall down a secret corridor. Finally they came to a great oak door, studded with rusty nails. When Virginia touched it, it swung back on its heavy hinges, and they found themselves in a little low room, with a vaulted ceiling and one tiny barred window. Imbedded in the wall was a huge iron ring, and chained to it was a skeleton that was stretched out at full length on the stone floor and seemed to be trying to grasp with its long fleshless fingers

chapter V

THE MONKEY'S PAW

ADAPTED FROM W. W. JACOBS

Without, the night was cold and wet, but in the small parlor of Lakesnam Villa the blinds were drawn and the fire burned brightly. Father and son were playing chess, the former, who possessed ideas about the game involving radical changes, putting his king into such sharp and unnecessary perils that it even provoked comment from the white-haired old lady knitting placidly by the fire.

"Hark at the wind," said Mr. White, who, having seen a fatal mistake after it was too late, was amiably desirous of preventing his son from seeing it.

"I'm listening," said the latter, grimly surveying the board as he stretched out his hand. "Check."

"I should hardly think that he'd come to-night," said his father, with his hand poised over the board.

"Mate," replied the son.

"That's the worst of living so far out," cried Mr. White, with sudden and unlooked-for temper; "of all the beastly, slushy, out-of-the-way places to live in, this is the worst. Pathway's a bog, and the road's a torrent. I don't know what people are thinking about. I suppose because only two houses on the road are sold, they think it doesn't matter."

"Never mind, dear," said his wife, soothingly; "perhaps you'll win the next one."

Mr. White looked up sharply, just in time to intercept a knowing glance between mother and son. The words died away on his lips, and he hid a guilty grin in his thin gray beard.

"There he is," said Herbert White, as the gate banged shut loudly and heavy footsteps came toward the door.

The old man rose with hospitable haste, and opening the door, was heard commiserating with the new arrival. The new arrival also commiserated with himself, so that Mrs. White said, "Tut, tut!" and coughed gently as her husband entered the room, followed by a tall burly man, beady of eye and rubicund of visage.

"Sergeant-Major Morris," he said, introducing him.

The sergeant-major shook hands, and taking the proffered seat by the fire, watched contentedly while his host got out whiskey and glasses and put a small copper kettle on the fire.

By the third glass his eyes got brighter, and he began to talk, the little family circle regarding with eager interest this visitor from distant parts, as he squared his broad shoulders in the chair and spoke of strange scenes and brave deeds, of wars and plagues and strange peoples.

"Twenty-one years of it," said Mr. White, nodding at his wife and son. "When he went away he was a slip of a youth in the warehouse. Now look at him."

"He don't look to have taken much harm," said Mrs. White, politely.

"I'd like to go to India myself," said the old man, "just to look round a bit, you know."

"Better where you are," said the sergeant-major, shaking his head. He put down the empty glass, and sighing softly, shook it again.

"I should like to see those old temples and fakirs and jugglers," said the old man. "What was that you started telling me the other day about a monkey's paw or something, Morris?"

"Nothing," said the soldier, hastily. "Leastways, nothing worth hearing."

"Monkey's paw?" said Mrs. White, curiously.

"Well, it's just a bit of what you might call magic, perhaps," said the sergeant-major, off handedly.

His three listeners leaned forward eagerly. The visitor absentmindedly put his empty glass to his lips and then set it down again. His host filled it for him.

"To look at," said the sergeant-major, fumbling in his pocket, "it's just an ordinary little paw, dried to a mummy."

He took something out of his pocket and proffered it. Mrs. White drew back with a grimace, but her son, taking it, examined it curiously.

"And what is there special about it?" inquired Mr. White as he took it from his son, and having examined it, placed it upon the table.

"It had a spell put on it by an old fakir," said the sergeant-major, "a very holy man. He wanted to show that fate ruled people's lives, and that those who interfered with it did so to their sorrow. He put a spell on it so that three separate men could each have three wishes from it."

His manner was so impressive that his hearers were conscious that their light laughter jarred somewhat.

"Well, why don't you have three, sir?" said Herbert White, cleverly.

The soldier regarded him in the way that middle age is wont to regard presumptuous youth. "I have," he said, quietly, and his blotchy face whitened.

"And did you really have the three wishes granted?" asked Mrs. White.

"I did," said the sergeant-major, and his glass tapped against his strong teeth.

"And has anybody else wished?" inquired the old lady.

"The first man had his three wishes, yes," was the reply. "I don't know what the first two were, but the third was for death. That's how I got the paw."

His tones were so grave that a hush fell upon the group.

"If you've had your three wishes, it's no good to you now, then, Morris," said the old man at last. "What do you keep it for?"

The soldier shook his head. "Whim, I suppose," he said, slowly. "I did have some idea of selling it, but I don't think I will. It has caused enough trouble already. Besides, people won't buy. They think it's a fairy-tale, some of them, and those who do think anything of it want to try it first and pay me afterward."

"If you could have another three wishes," said the old man, eying him keenly, "would you have them?"

"I don't know," said the other. "I don't know."

He took the paw, and dangling it between his front finger and thumb,

suddenly threw it upon the fire. White, with a slight cry, stooped down and snatched it off.

"Better let it burn," said the soldier, solemnly.

"If you don't want it, Morris," said the old man, "give it to me."

"I won't," said his friend, doggedly. "I threw it on the fire. If you keep it, don't blame me for what happens. Pitch it on the fire again, like a sensible man."

The other shook his head and examined his new possession closely. "How do you do it?" he inquired.

"Hold it up in your right hand and wish aloud," said the sergeant-major, "but I warn you of the consequences."

"Sounds like the *Arabian Nights*," said Mrs. White, as she rose and began to set the supper table. "Don't you think you might wish for four pairs of hands for me?"

Her husband drew the talisman from his pocket, and then all three burst into laughter as the sergeant-major, with a look of alarm on his face, caught him by the arm.

"If you must wish," he said, gruffly, "wish for something sensible."

Mr. White dropped it back into his pocket, and placing chairs, motioned his friend to the table. In the business of supper the talisman was partly forgotten, and afterward the three sat listening, enthralled, to a second installment of the soldier's adventures in India.

"If the tale about the monkey's paw is not more truthful than those he has been telling us," said Herbert, as the door closed behind their guest, just in time for him to catch the last train, "we shan't make much out of it."

"Did you give him anything for it, dear?" inquired Mrs. White, regarding her husband closely.

"A trifle," said he, coloring slightly. "He didn't want it, but I made him take it. And he pressed me again to throw it away."

"Likely," said Herbert, with pretended horror. "Why, we're going to be rich, and famous, and happy. Wish to be an emperor, Father, to begin with; then you can't be henpecked."

He darted round the table, pursued by the maligned Mrs. White armed with a dishrag.

Mr. White took the paw from his pocket and eyed it dubiously. "I don't know what to wish for, and that's a fact," he said, slowly. "It seems to me I've got all I want."

"If you only paid off the mortgage on the house, you'd be quite happy, wouldn't you?" said Herbert, with his hand on his shoulder. "Well, wish for two hundred pounds, then; that'll just do it."

His father, smiling shamefacedly at his own credulity, held up the talisman, as his son, with a solemn face somewhat marred by a wink at his mother, sat down at the piano and struck a few impressive chords.

"I wish for two hundred pounds," said the old man, distinctly.

A fine crash from the piano greeted the words, interrupted by a shuddering cry from the old man. His wife and son ran toward him.

"It moved," he cried, with a glance of disgust at the object as it lay on the floor. "As I wished, it twisted in my hands like a snake."

"Well, I don't see the money," said his son as he picked it up and placed it on the table, "and I bet I never shall."

"It must have been your imagination, Father," said his wife, regarding him anxiously.

He shook his head. "Never mind, though; there's no harm done, but it gave me a shock all the same."

They sat down by the fire again while the two men finished their pipes. Outside, the wind was higher than ever, and the old man started nervously at the sound of a door banging upstairs. A silence unusual and depressing settled upon all three, which lasted until the old couple rose to retire for the night.

"I expect you'll find the cash tied up in a big bag in the middle of your bed," said Herbert, as he bade them good-night, "and something horrible squatting up on top of the wardrobe watching you as you pocket your ill-gotten gains."

In the brightness of the wintry sun next morning as it streamed over the breakfast table, Herbert laughed at his fears. There was an air of cheerfulness about the room which it had lacked on the previous night, and the dirty, shriveled little paw was pitched on the sideboard with a carelessness which betokened no great belief in its virtues.

"I suppose all old soldiers are the same," said Mrs. White. "The idea of our listening to such nonsense! How could wishes be granted in these days? And if they could, how could two hundred pounds hurt you, Father?"

"Might drop on his head from the sky," said the jocular Herbert.

"Morris said the things happened so naturally," said his father, "that you might, if you so wished, attribute it to coincidence."

"Well, don't break into the money before I come back," said Herbert as he rose from the table. "I'm afraid it'll turn you into a mean, avaricious man, and we shall have to disown you."

His mother laughed, and following him to the door, watched him down the road, and returning to the breakfast table, was very happy at the expense of her husband's credulity. All of which did not prevent her from scurrying to the door at the postman's knock, nor prevent her from referring somewhat shortly to retired sergeant-majors of bibulous habits when she found that the post brought a tailor's bill.

"Herbert will have some more of his funny remarks, I expect, when he comes home," she said as they sat at dinner.

"I daresay," said Mr. White, pouring himself out some beer; "but for all that, the thing moved in my hand; that I'll swear to."

"You thought it did," said the old lady, soothingly.

"I say it did," replied the other. "There was no thought about it; I had just— What's the matter?"

His wife made no reply. She was watching the mysterious movements of a man outside, who, peering in an undecided fashion at the house, appeared to be trying to make up his mind to enter. In mental connection with the two hundred pounds, she noticed that the stranger was well dressed and wore a silk hat of glossy newness. Three times he paused at the gate, and then walked on again. The fourth time he stood with his hand upon it, and then with sudden resolution flung it open and walked up the path.

Answering his knock at the door, Mrs. White brought the stranger, who seemed ill at ease, into the room. He looked furtively at Mrs. White, and listened in a preoccupied fashion as the old lady apologized for the appearance of the room, and her husband's coat, a garment which he usually reserved for the garden. She then waited patiently for him to state his business, but he was at first strangely silent.

"I—was asked to call," he said at last, and stooped and picked a piece of cotton from his trousers. "I come from Maw and Meggins."

The old lady started. "Is anything the matter?" she asked, breathlessly. "Has anything happened to Herbert? What is it? What is it?"

Her husband interposed. "There, there, Mother," he said, hastily. "Sit down, and don't jump to conclusions. You've not brought bad news, I'm sure, sir," and he eyed the other pensively.

"I'm sorry—" began the visitor.

"Is he hurt?" demanded the mother.

The visitor bowed in assent. "Badly hurt," he said, quietly, "but he is not in any pain."

"Oh, thank God!" said the old woman, clasping her hands. "Thank God for that! Thank—"

She broke off suddenly as the sinister meaning of the assurance dawned upon her and she saw the awful confirmation of her fears in the other's averted face. She caught her breath, and turning to her slower-witted husband, laid her trembling old hand upon his. There was a long silence.

"He was caught in the machinery," said the visitor at length in a low voice.

"Caught in the machinery," repeated Mr. White in a dazed fashion, "yes."

He sat staring blankly out at the window, and taking his wife's hand between his own, pressed it as he had been wont to do in their old courting days nearly forty years before.

"He was the only one left to us," he said, turning gently to the visitor. "It is hard."

The other coughed, and rising, walked slowly to the window. "The firm wished me to convey their sincere sympathy with you in your great loss," he said, without looking round. "I beg that you will understand I am only their servant and merely obeying orders."

There was no reply; the old woman's face was white, her eyes staring, and her breath inaudible; on the husband's face was a look such as his friend the sergeant might have carried into his first action.

"I was to say that Maw and Meggins disclaim all responsibility," continued the other. "They admit no liability at all, but in consideration of your son's service they wish to present you with a certain sum as compensation."

Mr. White dropped his wife's hand, and rising to his feet, gazed with a look of horror at his visitor. His dry lips shaped the words, "How much?"

"Two hundred pounds" was the answer.

Unconscious of his wife's shriek, the old man smiled faintly, put out his hands like a sightless man, and dropped, a senseless heap, to the floor.

In the huge new cemetery, some two miles distant, the old people buried their dead, and came back to a house steeped in shadow and silence. It was all over so quickly that at first they could hardly realize it, and remained in a state of expectation as though of something else to happen—something else which was to lighten this load, too heavy for old hearts to bear.

But the days passed, and expectation gave place to resignation—the hopeless resignation of the old, sometimes miscalled apathy. Sometimes they hardly exchanged a word, for now they had nothing to talk about, and their days were long to weariness.

It was about a week after that that the old man, waking suddenly in the night, stretched out his hand and found himself alone. The room was in darkness, and the sound of subdued weeping came from the window. He raised himself in bed and listened.

"Come back," he said, tenderly. "You will be cold."

"It is colder for my son," said the old woman, and wept again.

The sound of her sobs died away on his ears. The bed was warm, and his eyes heavy with sleep. He dozed fitfully, and then slept until a sudden wild cry from his wife awoke him with a start.

"The monkey's paw!" she cried, wildly. "The monkey's paw!"

He started up in alarm. "Where? Where is it? What's the matter?"

She came stumbling across the room toward him. "I want it," she said, quietly. "You've not destroyed it?"

"It's in the parlor, on the mantel," he replied, bewildered. "Why?"

She cried and laughed together, and bending over, kissed his cheek.

"I only just thought of it," she said, hysterically. "Why didn't I think of it before? Why didn't you think of it?"

"Think of what?" he questioned.

"The other two wishes," she replied, rapidly. "We've only had one."

"Was not that enough?" he demanded, fiercely.

"No," she cried, triumphantly; "we'll have one more. Go down and get it quickly, and wish our boy alive again."

The man sat up in bed and flung the bedclothes from his quaking limbs. "Good God, you are mad!" he cried, aghast.

"Get it," she panted; "get it quickly, and wish— Oh, my boy, my boy!"

Her husband struck a match and lit the candle. "Get back to bed," he said, unsteadily. "You don't know what you are saying."

"We had the first wish granted," said the old woman, feverishly; "why not the second?"

"A coincidence," stammered the old man.

"Go and get it and wish," cried the old woman, and dragged him toward the door.

He went down in the darkness, and felt his way to the parlor, and then to the mantel-piece. The talisman was in its place, and a horrible fear that the unspoken wish might bring his mutilated son before him ere he could escape from the room seized upon him, and he caught his breath as he found that he had lost the direction of the door. His brow cold with sweat, he felt his way round the table, and groped along the wall until he found himself in the small passage with the unwholesome thing in his hand.

Even his wife's face seemed changed as he entered the room. It was white and expectant, and to his fears seemed to have an unnatural look upon it. He was afraid of her.

"Wish!" she cried, in a strong voice.

"It is foolish and wicked," he faltered.

"Wish!" repeated his wife.

He raised his hand. "I wish my son alive again."

The talisman fell to the floor, and he regarded it with a shudder. Then he sank trembling into a chair as the old woman, with burning eyes, walked to the window and raised the blind.

He sat until he was chilled with the cold, glancing occasionally at the figure of the old woman peering through the window. The candle end, which had burned below the rim of the china candlestick, was throwing pulsating shadows on the ceiling and walls, until, with a flicker larger than the rest, it expired. The old man, with an unspeakable sense of relief at the failure of the talisman, crept back to his bed, and a minute or two afterward the old woman came silently and apathetically beside him.

Neither spoke, but both lay silently listening to the ticking of the clock. A stair creaked, and a squeaky mouse scurried noisily through the wall. The darkness was oppressive, and after lying for some time screwing up his courage, the husband took the box of matches, and striking one, went downstairs for a candle.

At the foot of the stairs the match went out, and he paused to strike another, and at the same moment a knock, so quiet and stealthy as to be scarcely audible, sounded on the front door.

The matches fell from his hand. He stood motionless, his breath suspended until the knock was repeated. Then he turned and fled swiftly back to his room, and closed the door behind him. A third knock sounded through the house.

"*What's that?*" cried the old woman, starting up.

"A rat," said the old man in shaking tones—"a rat. It passed me on the stairs."

His wife sat up in bed listening. A loud knock resounded through the house.

"It's Herbert!" she screamed. "It's Herbert!"

She ran to the door, but her husband was before her, and catching her by the arm, held her tightly.

"What are you going to do?" he whispered hoarsely.

"It's my boy; it's Herbert!" she cried, struggling mechanically. "I forgot it was two miles away. What are you holding me for? Let go. I must open the door."

"For God's sake don't let it in," cried the old man, trembling.

"You're afraid of your own son," she cried, struggling. "Let me go. I'm coming, Herbert; I'm coming."

There was another knock, and another. The old woman with a sudden wrench broke free and ran from the room. Her husband followed to the landing, and called after her urgently as she hurried down the stairs. He heard the chain rattle back and the bottom bolt drawn slowly and stiffly from the socket. Then the old woman's voice, strained and panting.

"The bolt," she cried loudly. "Come down. I can't reach it."

But her husband was on his hands and knees groping wildly on the floor in search of the paw. If he could only find it before the thing outside got in. A perfect fusillade of knocks reverberated through the house, and he heard the scraping of a chair as his wife put it down in the passage against the door. He heard the creaking of the bolt as it came slowly back, and at the same moment he found the monkey's paw, and frantically breathed his third and last wish.

The knocking ceased suddenly, although the echoes of it were still in the house. He heard the chair drawn back and the door opened. A cold wind rushed up the staircase, and a long loud wail of disappointment and misery from his wife gave him courage to run down to her side, and then to the gate beyond. The street lamp flickering opposite shone on a quiet and deserted road.

chapter VI

THE STORY OF THE
INEXPERIENCED GHOST

ADAPTED FROM H. G. WELLS

The scene amid which clayton told his last story comes back very vividly to my mind. There he sat, for the greater part of the time, in the corner of the hearth by the spacious open fire, and Sanderson sat beside him smoking his pipe. There was Evans, and that marvel among actors, Wish, who is also a modest man. We had all come down to the Mermaid Club that Saturday morning, except Clayton, who had slept there overnight—which indeed gave him the opening of his story. We had golfed until golfing was invisible; we had dined, and we were in that mood of tranquil kindliness when men will suffer a story. When Clayton began to tell one, we naturally supposed he was lying. It may be that indeed he was lying—of that the reader will speedily be able to judge as well as I. He began, it is true, with an air of matter-of-fact anecdote, but that we thought was only the incurable artifice of the man.

"I say!" he remarked, after a long consideration of the upward rain of sparks from the log that Sanderson had thumped, "you know I was alone here last night?"

"Except for the servants," said Wish.

"Who sleep in the other wing," said Clayton. "Yes. Well—" He pulled at his cigar for some little time as though he still hesitated about his confidence. Then he said, quite quietly, "I caught a ghost!"

"Caught a ghost, did you?" said Sanderson. "Where is it?"

And Evans, who admires Clayton immensely and has been four weeks in America, shouted, "*Caught* a ghost, did you, Clayton? I'm glad of it! Tell us all about it right now."

Clayton said he would in a minute, and asked him to shut the door.

He looked apologetically at me. "There's no eavesdropping, of course, but we don't want to upset our very excellent help with any rumors of ghosts in the place. There's too much shadow and dark oak paneling as it is to trifle with that. And this, you know, wasn't a regular ghost. I don't think it will come again—ever."

"You mean to say you didn't keep it?" said Sanderson.

"I hadn't the heart to," said Clayton.

And Sanderson said he was surprised.

We laughed, and Clayton looked aggrieved. "I know," he said, with the flicker of a smile, "but the fact is it really *was* a ghost, and I'm as sure of it as I am that I am talking to you now. I'm not joking. I mean what I say."

Sanderson drew deeply at his pipe, with one reddish eye on Clayton, and then emitted a thin jet of smoke more eloquent than many words.

Clayton ignored the comment. "It is the strangest thing that has ever happened in my life. You know, I never believed in ghosts or anything of the sort, before, ever; and then, you know, I bag one in a corner; and the whole business is in my hands."

He meditated still more profoundly, and produced and began to pierce a second cigar with a curious little stabber he brought from his pocket.

"You talked to it?" asked Wish.

"For the space, probably, of an hour."

"Chatty?" I said, joining the party of the skeptics.

"The poor devil was in trouble," said Clayton, bowed over his cigar-end and with the very faintest note of reproof.

"Sobbing?" someone asked.

Clayton heaved a realistic sigh at the memory. "Good Lord!" he said; "yes." And then, "Poor fellow! yes."

"Where did you strike it?" asked Evans, in his best American accent.

"I never realized," said Clayton, ignoring him, "the poor sort of thing a ghost might be," and he hung us up again for a time, while he sought for matches in his pocket and lit and puffed on his cigar.

"I took an advantage," he reflected at last.

We were none of us in a hurry. "A character," he said, "remains just the same character for all that it's been disembodied. That's a thing we too often forget. People with a certain strength or fixity of purpose may have ghosts of a certain strength and fixity of purpose—most haunting ghosts, you know, must be as one-idea'd as monomaniacs and as obstinate as mules to come back again and again. This poor creature wasn't." He suddenly looked up rather queerly, and his eye went round the room. "I say it," he said, "in all kindliness, but that is the plain truth of the case. Even at the first glance he struck me as weak."

He punctuated with the help of his cigar.

"I came upon him, you know, in the long passage. His back was toward me and I saw him first. Right off I knew him for a ghost. He was transparent and whitish; clean through his chest I could see the glimmer of the little window at the end. And not only his physique but his attitude struck me as being weak. He looked, you know, as though he didn't know in the slightest whatever he meant to do. One hand was on the paneling and the other fluttered to his mouth. Like—SO!"

"What sort of physique?" said Sanderson.

"Lean. You know that sort of young man's neck that has two great flutings down the back, here and here—so! And a little, paltry head with scrubby hair— And rather bad ears. Shoulders bad, narrower than the hips; turndown collar, ready-made jacket, trousers baggy and a little frayed at the heels. That's how he struck me. I came very quietly up the staircase. I did not carry a light, you know—the candles are on the landing table and there is that lamp—and I was in my lounging slippers, and I saw him as I came up. I stopped dead at that—taking him in. I wasn't a bit afraid. I think that in most of these affairs one is never nearly so afraid or excited as one imagines one would be. I was surprised and interested. I thought, 'Good Lord! Here's a ghost at last! And I haven't believed for a moment in ghosts during the last five-and-twenty years.'"

"Um," said Wish.

"I suppose I wasn't on the landing a moment before he found out I was there. He turned on me sharply, and I saw the face of an immature young man, a weak nose, a scrubby little moustache, a feeble chin. So for an instant we stood—he looking over his shoulder at me, and we regarded one another. Then he seemed to remember his high calling. He turned round, drew himself up, projected his face, raised his arms, spread his hands in approved ghost fashion—came toward me. As he did so his little jaw dropped, and he emitted a faint, drawn-out 'Boo.' No, it wasn't—not a bit dreadful. I'd dined. I'd had a bottle of champagne, and being all alone, perhaps two or three—perhaps even four or five—whiskeys, so I was as solid as a rock and no more frightened than if I'd been assailed by a frog. 'Boo!' I said. 'Nonsense. You don't belong to *this* place. What are you doing here?'

"I could see him wince. 'Boo-oo,' he said.

"'Boo—be hanged! Are you a member?' I said; and just to show I didn't care a pin for him I stepped through a corner of him and made to light my candle. 'Are you a member?' I repeated, looking at him sideways.

"He moved a little so as to stand clear of me, and his bearing became crestfallen. 'No,' he said, in answer to the persistent interrogation of my eye; 'I'm not a member—I'm a ghost.'

"'Well, that doesn't give you the run of the Mermaid Club. Is there anyone you want to see, or anything of that sort?' and doing it as steadily as possible for fear that he should mistake the carelessness of whiskey for the distraction of fear, I got my candle alight. I turned on him, holding it. 'What are you doing here?' I said.

"He had dropped his hands and stopped his booing, and there he stood,

abashed and awkward, the ghost of a weak, silly, aimless young man. 'I'm haunting,' he said.

"'You haven't any business to,' I said in a quiet voice.

"'I'm a ghost,' he said, as if in defense.

"'That may be, but you haven't any business to haunt here. This is a respectable private club; people often stop here with nursemaids and children, and, going about in the careless way you do, some poor little mite could easily come upon you and be scared out of her wits. I suppose you didn't think of that?'

"'No, sir,' he said, 'I didn't.'

"'You should have done. You haven't any claim on the place, have you? Weren't murdered here, or anything of that sort?'

"'None, sir; but I thought as it was old and oak-paneled—'

"'That's *no* excuse.' I regarded him firmly. 'Your coming here is a mistake,' I said, in a tone of friendly superiority. I feigned to see if I had my matches, and then looked up at him frankly. 'If I were you I wouldn't wait for cock-crow— I'd vanish right away.'

"He looked embarrassed. 'The fact *is*, sir—' he began.

"'I'd vanish,' I said, driving it home.

"'The fact is, sir, that—somehow—I can't.'

"'You *can't?*'

"'No, sir. There's something I've forgotten. I've been hanging about here since midnight last night, hiding in the cupboards of the empty bedrooms and things like that. I'm flustered. I've never come haunting before, and it seems to put me out.'

"'Put you out?'

"'Yes, sir. I've tried to do it several times, and it doesn't come off. There's some little thing I've forgotten, and I can't get back.'

"That, you know, rather bowled me over. He looked at me in such an abject way that for the life of me I couldn't keep up quite the high, hectoring vein I had adopted. 'That's queer,' I said, and as I spoke I fancied I heard someone moving about down below. 'Come into my room and tell me more about it,' I said. 'I didn't, of course, understand this,' and I tried to take him by the arm. But, of course, you might as well have tried to take hold of a puff of smoke! I had forgotten my room number, I think; anyhow, I remember going into several bedrooms—it was lucky I was the only soul in that wing—until I saw my luggage. 'Here we are,' I said, and sat down in the arm-chair; 'sit down and tell me all about it. It seems to me you have got yourself into a jolly awkward position, old chap.'

"Well, he said he wouldn't sit down! He'd prefer to flit up and down the room if it was all the same to me. And so he did, and in a little while we were deep in a long and serious talk. And presently, you know, something of those whiskeys and sodas evaporated out of me, and I began to realize just a little what a thundering bad and weird business it was that I was in. There he was, semi-transparent—the proper conventional phantom, and noiseless except for his ghost of a voice—flitting to and fro in that nice, clean, chintz-hung old bedroom. You could see the gleam of the copper candlesticks through him, and the lights on the brass fender, and the corners of the framed engravings on the wall—and there he was telling me all about this wretched little life of

his that had recently ended on earth. He hadn't a particularly honest face, you know, but being transparent, of course, he couldn't avoid telling the truth."

"Eh?" said Wish, suddenly sitting up in his chair.

"What?" said Clayton.

"Being transparent—couldn't avoid telling the truth—I don't see it," said Wish.

"*I* don't see it," said Clayton, with inimitable assurance. "But it *is* so, I can assure you nevertheless. I don't believe he got once a nail's breadth off the Bible truth. He told me how he had been killed—he went down into a London basement with a candle to look for a leakage of gas—and described himself as a senior English master in a London private school when that release occurred."

"Poor wretch!" said I.

"That's what I thought, and the more he talked, the more I thought it. There he was, purposeless in life and purposeless out of it. He talked of his father and mother and his schoolmaster, and all who had ever been anything to him in the world, pathetically. He had been too sensitive, too nervous; none of them had ever valued him properly or understood him, he said. He had never had a real friend in the world, I think; he had never had a success. He had shirked games and failed examinations. 'It's like that with some people,' he said; 'whenever I got into the examination-room or anywhere, everything seemed to go.' Engaged to be married, of course—to another over-sensitive person, I suppose—when the indiscretion with the gas escape ended his affairs. 'And where are you now?' I asked. 'Not in—?'

"He wasn't clear on that point at all. The impression he gave me was of a sort of vague, intermediate state, a special reserve for souls too nonexistent for anything so positive as either sin or virtue. *I* don't know. He was much too egotistical and unobservant to give me any clear idea of the kind of place, kind of country, there is on the Other Side of Things. Wherever he was, he seems to have fallen in with a set of kindred spirits: ghosts of weak Cockney young men, who were on a footing of first names, and among these there was certainly a lot of talk about 'going haunting' and things like that. Yes—going haunting! They seemed to think 'haunting' a tremendous adventure, though most of them were afraid to do it. And so primed, you know, he had come."

"But really!" said Wish to the fire.

"These are the impressions he gave me, anyhow," said Clayton, modestly. "I may, of course, have been in a rather uncritical state, but that was the sort of background he gave to himself. He kept flitting up and down, with his thin voice going talking, talking about his wretched self, and never a word of clear, firm statement from first to last. He was thinner and sillier and more pointless than if he had been real and alive. Only then, you know, he would not have been in my bedroom here—if he *had* been alive. I should have kicked him out."

"Of course," said Evans, "there *are* poor mortals like that."

"And there's just as much chance of their having ghosts as the rest of us," I admitted.

"What gave a sort of point to him, you know, was the fact that he did seem within limits to have found himself out. The mess he had made of haunting had depressed him terribly. He had been told it would be a 'lark'; he had come expecting it to be a 'lark,' and here it was, nothing but another failure added to his record! He proclaimed himself an utter out-and-out failure. He said, and I can quite believe it, that he had never tried to do anything all his life that he hadn't made a perfect mess of—and through all the wastes of eternity he never would. If he had had sympathy, perhaps— He paused at that, and stood regarding me. He remarked that, strange as it might seem to me, nobody, not anyone, ever, had given him the amount of sympathy I was doing now. I could see what he wanted straightaway, and I determined to head him off at once. I may be a brute, you know, but being the Only Real Friend, the recipient of the confidences of one of these egotistical weaklings, ghost or body, is beyond my physical endurance. I got up briskly. 'Don't you brood on these things too much,' I said. 'The thing you've got to do is to get out of this, get out of this— sharp. You pull yourself together and *try*.' 'I can't,' he said. 'You try,' I said, and try he did."

"Try!" said Sanderson. *"How?"*

"Passes," said Clayton.

"Passes?"

"Complicated series of gestures and passes with the hands. That's how he had come in and that's how he had to get out again. Lord! what a business I had!"

"But how could *any* series of passes—?" I began.

"My dear man," said Clayton, turning on me and putting a great emphasis on certain words, "you want *everything* clear. *I* don't know *how*. All I know is that you *do*—that *he* did, anyhow, at least. After a fearful time, you know, he got his passes right and suddenly disappeared."

"Did you," said Sanderson, slowly, "observe the passes?"

"Yes," said Clayton, and seemed to think. "It was tremendously queer," he said. "There we were, I and this thin vague ghost, in that silent room, in this silent, empty inn, in this silent little Friday-night town. Not a sound except our voices and a faint panting he made when he swung. There was the bedroom candle, and one candle on the dressing-table alight, that was all—sometimes one or other would flare up into a tall, lean, astonished flame for a space. And queer things happened. 'I can't,' he said; 'I shall never—!' And suddenly he sat down on a little chair at the foot of the bed and began to sob and sob. Lord! what a harrowing, whimpering thing he seemed!

"'You pull yourself together,' I said, and tried to pat him on the back, and . . . my confounded hand went through him! By that time, you know, I wasn't nearly so—impassive as I had been on the landing. I got the queerness of it full. I remember snatching back my hand out of him, as it were, with a little thrill, and walking over to the dressing-table. 'You pull yourself together,' I said to him, 'and try.' And in order to encourage and help him I began to try as well."

"What!" said Sanderson, "the passes?"

"Yes, the passes."

"But—" I said, moved by an idea that eluded me for a space.

"This is interesting," said Sanderson, with his finger in his pipe-bowl. "You mean to say this ghost of yours gave away—"

"Did his level best to give away the whole confounded barrier? Yes."

"He didn't," said Wish; "he couldn't. Or you'd have gone there too."

"That's precisely it," I said, finding my elusive idea put into words for me.

"That *is* precisely it," said Clayton, with thoughtful eyes upon the fire.

For just a little while there was silence.

"And at last he did it?" said Sanderson.

"At last he did it. I had to keep him hard at it, but he did it at last—rather suddenly. He despaired, we had a scene, and then he got up abruptly and asked me to go through the whole performance, slowly, so that he might see. 'I believe,' he said, 'if I could *see* I should spot what was wrong at once.' And he did. '*I* know,' he said. 'What do you know?' said I. '*I* know,' he repeated. Then he said, peevishly, 'I *can't* do it if you look at me—I really *can't*; it's been that, partly, all along. I'm such a nervous fellow that you put me out.' Well, we had a bit of an argument. Naturally I wanted to see; but he was as obstinate as a mule, and suddenly I had come over as tired as a dog—he tired me out. 'All right,' I said, '*I* won't look at you,' and turned toward the mirror, on the wardrobe, by the bed.

He started off very fast. I tried to follow him by looking in the looking-glass, to see just what it was had gone wrong. Round went his arms and his hands, so, and so, and so, and then with a rush came to the last gesture of all—you stand erect and open out your arms—and so, don't you know, he stood. And then he didn't! He didn't! He wasn't! I wheeled round from the looking-glass to him. There was nothing. I was alone, with the flaring candles and a staggering mind. What had happened? Had anything happened? Had I been dreaming? . . . And then, with an absurd note of finality about it, the clock upon the landing discovered the moment was ripe for striking *one*. So!—Ping! And I was as grave and sober as a judge, with all my champagne and whiskey gone into the vast serene. Feeling queer, you know—confoundedly queer! Queer! Good Lord!"

He regarded his cigar-ash for a moment. "That's all that happened," he said.

"And then you went to bed?" asked Evans.

"What else was there to do?"

I looked Wish in the eye. We wanted to scoff, and there was something, something perhaps in Clayton's voice and manner, that hampered our desire.

"And about these gestures?" said Sanderson.

"I believe I could do them now."

"Oh!" said Sanderson, and produced a pen-knife and set himself to ream out the bowl of his pipe.

"Why don't you do them now?" said Sanderson, shutting his pen-knife with a click.

"That's what I'm going to do," said Clayton.

"They won't work," said Evans.

"If they do—" I suggested.

"You know, I'd rather you didn't," said Wish, stretching out his legs.

"Why?" asked Evans.

"I'd rather he didn't," said Wish.

"But he hasn't got 'em right," said Sanderson, plugging too much tobacco in his pipe.

"All the same, I'd rather he didn't," said Wish.

We argued with Wish. He said that for Clayton to go through those gestures was like mocking a serious matter. "But you don't believe——?" I said. Wish glanced at Clayton, who was staring into the fire, weighing something in his mind. "I do—more than half, anyhow, I do," said Wish.

"Clayton," said I, "you're too good a liar for us. Most of it was all right. But that disappearance . . . happened to be convincing. Tell us, it's a tale of cock and bull."

He stood up without heeding me, took the middle of the hearthrug, and faced me. For a moment he regarded his feet thoughtfully, and then for all the rest of the time his eyes were on the opposite wall, with an intent expression. He raised his two hands slowly to the level of his eyes and so began. . . .

Now, Sanderson is a Freemason, a member of the lodge of the Four Kings, which devotes itself so ably to the study and elucidation of all the mysteries of Masonry past and present, and among the students of this lodge Sanderson is by no means the least. He followed Clayton's motions with a singular interest in his reddish eye. "That's not bad," he said, when it was done. "You really do, you know, put things together, Clayton, in a most amazing fashion. But there's one little detail out."

"I know," said Clayton. "I believe I could tell you which."

"Well?"

"This," said Clayton, and did a queer little twist and writhing and thrust of the hands.

"Yes."

"That, you know, was what *he* couldn't get right," said Clayton. "But how do you—?"

"Most of this business, and particularly how you came to it, I don't understand at all," said Sanderson, "but just that phase—I do." He reflected. "These happen to be a series of gestures—connected with a certain branch of esoteric Masonry. Probably you know. Or else—*how?*" He reflected still further. "I do not see I can do any harm in telling you just the proper twist. After all, if you know, you know; if you don't, you don't."

"I know nothing," said Clayton, "except what the poor devil did last night."

"Well, anyhow," said Sanderson, and placed his briar very carefully upon the shelf over the fireplace. Then very rapidly he gesticulated with his hands.

"So?" said Clayton, repeating.

"So," said Sanderson, and took his pipe in hand again.

"Ah, *now*," said Clayton, "I can do the whole thing—right."

He stood up before the waning fire and smiled at us all. But I think there was just a little hesitation in his smile. "If I begin—" he said.

"I wouldn't begin," said Wish.

"It's all right!" said Evans. "Matter is indestructible. You don't think any jiggery-pokery of this sort is going to snatch Clayton into the world of shades. Not a chance! You may try, Clayton, so far as I'm concerned, until your arms drop off at the wrists."

"I don't believe that," said Wish, and stood up and put his arm on Clayton's shoulder. "You've made me half believe in that story somehow, and I don't want to see the thing done!"

"Goodness!" said I. "Here's Wish frightened!"

"I am," said Wish, with real or admirably feigned intensity. "I believe that if he goes through these motions right he'll go."

"He'll not do anything of the sort," I cried. "There's only one way out of this world for men, and Clayton is thirty years from that. Besides . . . And such a ghost! Do you think—?"

Wish interrupted me by moving. He walked out from among our chairs and stopped beside the table and stood there. "Clayton," he said, "you're a fool."

Clayton, with a humorous light in his eyes, smiled back at him. "Wish," he said, "is right and all you others are wrong. I shall go. I shall get to the end of these passes, and as the last swish whistles through the air, Presto!—this hearthrug will be vacant, the room will be blank amazement, and a respectably dressed gentleman of two hundred pounds will plump into the world of shades. I'm certain. So will you be. I decline to argue further. Let the thing be tried."

"*No,*" said Wish, and made a step and ceased, and Clayton raised his hands once more to repeat the spirit's passing.

By that time, you know, we were all in a state of tension—largely because of the behavior of Wish. We sat all of us with our eyes on Clayton—I, at least, with a sort of tight, stiff feeling about me as though from the back of my skull to the middle of my thighs my body had been changed to steel. And there, with a gravity that was imperturbably serene, Clayton bowed and swayed and waved his hands and arms before us. As he drew toward the end, one shivered, one tingled in one's teeth. The last gesture, I have said, was to swing the arms out wide open, with the face held up. And when at last he swung out to this closing gesture I ceased even to breathe. It was ridiculous, of course, but you know that ghost-story feeling. It was after dinner, in a queer, old shadowy house. Would he, after all——?

There he stood for one stupendous moment, with his arms open and his upturned face, assured and bright, in the glare of the hanging lamp. We hung through that moment as if it were an age, and then came from all of us something that was half a sigh of infinite relief and half a reassuring *"No!"* For visibly—he wasn't going. It was all nonsense. He had told an idle story, and carried it almost to conviction, that was all! . . . And then in

that moment the face of Clayton changed.

It changed. It changed as a lit house changes when its lights are suddenly extinguished. His eyes were suddenly eyes that were fixed, his smile was frozen on his lips, and he stood there still. He stood there, very gently swaying.

That moment, too, was an age. And then, you know, chairs were scraping, things were falling, and we were all moving. His knees seemed to give, and he fell forward, and Evans rose and caught him in his arms. . . .

It stunned us all. For a minute I suppose no one said a coherent thing. We believed it, yet could not believe it. . . . I came out of a muddled stupefaction to find myself kneeling beside him, and his vest and shirt were torn open, and Sanderson's hand lay on his heart. . . .

Well—the simple fact before us could very well wait our convenience; there was no hurry for us to comprehend. It lay there for an hour; it lies athwart my memory, black and amazing still, to this day. Clayton had, indeed, passed into the world that lies so near to and so far from our own, and he had gone thither by the only road that mortal man may take. But whether he did indeed pass there by that poor ghost's incantation, or whether he was stricken suddenly by apoplexy in the midst of an idle tale—as the coroner's jury would have us believe—is no matter for my judging; it is just one of those inexplicable riddles that must remain unsolved until the final solution of all things shall come. All I certainly know is that, in the very moment, in the very instant, of concluding those passes, he changed, and staggered, and fell down before us—dead!

chapter VII

A DIAGNOSIS OF DEATH

ADAPTED FROM AMBROSE BIERCE

"I am not so superstitious as some of you physicians—men of science, as you are pleased to be called," said Hawver, replying to an accusation that had not been made. "Some of you—only a few, I confess—believe in the immortality of the soul, and in apparitions which you have not the honesty to call ghosts. I go no further than a conviction that the living are sometimes seen where they are not, but have been—where they have lived so long, perhaps so intensely, as to have left their impress on everything about them. I know, indeed, that one's environment may be so affected by one's personality as to yield, long afterward, an image of one's self to the eyes of another. Doubtless the impressing personality has to be the right kind of personality, as the perceiving eyes have to be the right kind of eyes—mine, for example."

"Yes, the right kind of eyes, conveying sensations to the wrong kind of brains," said Dr. Frayley, smiling.

"Thank you; one likes to have an expectation gratified; that is about the reply that I supposed you would have the civility to make."

"Pardon me. But you say that you know about these, er, ghosts. That is

do with what I have to tell; I thought it might amuse a physician.

"The house was furnished, just as he had lived in it. It was a rather gloomy dwelling for one who was neither a recluse nor a student, and I think it gave something of its character to me—perhaps some of its former occupant's character; for always I felt in it a certain melancholy that was not in my natural disposition, nor, I think, due to loneliness. I had no servants that slept in the house, but I have always been, as you know, rather fond of my own company, being much addicted to reading, though little to study. Whatever was the cause, the effect was dejection and a sense of impending evil; this was especially so in Dr. Mannering's study, although that room was the lightest and most airy in the house. The doctor's life-size portrait in oil hung in that room, and seemed completely to dominate it. There was nothing unusual in the picture; the man was evidently rather good-looking, about fifty years old, with iron-gray hair, a bushy mustache, and dark, serious eyes. Something in the picture always drew and held my attention. The man's appearance became familiar to me, and rather 'haunted' me.

"One evening I was passing through this room to my bedroom, with a lamp—there is no gas in Meridian. I stopped as usual before the portrait, which seemed in the lamplight to have a new expression, not easily named, but distinctly uncanny. It interested but did not disturb me. I moved the lamp from one side to the other and observed the effects of the altered light. While so engaged I felt an impulse to turn round. As I did so I saw a man moving across the room directly toward me! As soon as he came near enough for the lamplight to illuminate the face, I saw that it was Dr. Mannering himself; it was as if the portrait were walking!

"'I beg your pardon,' I said, somewhat coldly, 'but if you knocked I did not hear.'

"He passed me, within an arm's length, lifted his right forefinger, as in warning, and without a word went on out of the room, though I observed his exit no more than I had observed his entrance.

"Of course, I need not tell you that this was what you will call an hallucination and I call an apparition. That room had only two doors, of which one was locked; the other led into a bedroom, from which there was no exit. My feeling on realizing this is not an important part of the incident.

"Doubtless this seems to you a very commonplace 'ghost story'—one constructed on the regular lines laid down by the old masters of the art. If that

were so, I should not have related it, even if it were true. The man was not dead; I met him today in Union Street. He passed me in a crowd."

Hawver had finished his story and both men were silent. Dr. Frayley absently drummed on the table with his fingers.

"Did he say anything today?" he asked—"anything from which you inferred that he was not dead?"

Hawver stared and did not reply.

"Perhaps," suggested Frayley, "he made a sign, a gesture—lifted a finger, as in warning. It's a trick he had—a habit when saying something serious—announcing the result of a diagnosis, for example."

"Yes, he did—just as his apparition had done. But, good God! do you know him?"

Hawver was apparently growing nervous.

"I knew him. I have read his book, as will every physician someday. It is one of the most striking and important of the century's contributions to medical science. Yes, I knew him; I attended him in an illness three years ago. He died."

Hawver sprang from his chair, manifestly disturbed. He strode forward and back across the room; then approached his friend, and in a voice not altogether steady, said: "Doctor, have you anything to say to me—as a physician?"

"No, Hawver; you are the healthiest man I ever knew. As a friend I advise you to go to your room. You play the violin like an angel. Play it; play something light and lively. Get this cursed bad business off your mind."

The next day Hawver was found dead in his room, the violin at his neck, the bow in his hands, his music open before him at Chopin's Funeral March.

chapter VIII

LAURA

ADAPTED FROM SAKI (H. H. MUNRO)

"You aren't really dying, are you?" asked Amanda.

"I have the doctor's permission to live till Tuesday," said Laura.

"But today is Saturday; this is serious!" gasped Amanda.

"I don't know about it being serious; it is certainly Saturday," said Laura.

"Death is always serious," said Amanda.

"I never said I was going to die. I am presumably going to leave off being Laura, but shall go on being something. An animal of some kind, I suppose. You see, when one hasn't been very good in the life one has just lived, one comes back as some lower organism. And I haven't been good when one comes to think of it. I've been petty and mean and vindictive and all that sort of thing when circumstances seem to call for it."

"Circumstances never call for that sort of thing," said Amanda reprovingly.

"If you don't mind my saying so," observed Laura, "Egbert is a circumstance that would call for any amount of that sort of thing. You're married to him—that's different; you've sworn to love, honor, and endure him: I haven't."

"I don't see what's wrong with Egbert," protested Amanda.

"Oh, I'm sure the fault has been mine," admitted Laura dispassionately;

"he has merely been the extenuating circumstance. He made a thin, peevish kind of fuss, for instance, when I took the collie puppies from the farm out for a run the other day."

"But they chased his young brood of Sussex speckled hens out of the hen-house and then trampled all over the flower beds," said Amanda. "You know how devoted he is to his chickens and garden."

"Anyhow, he needn't have gone on about it for the whole evening and then have said, 'Let's say no more about it,' just when I was beginning to enjoy the discussion. That's where one of my petty vindictive revenges came in," added Laura with an unrepentant chuckle; "I chased the entire family of Sussex speckled hens into his seedling shed the day after the puppy episode."

"How could you?" exclaimed Amanda. "And we thought it was an accident!"

"You see," resumed Laura, "I really have some grounds for supposing that my next incarnation will be in a lower organism. I shall be an animal of some kind. On the other hand, I haven't been a bad sort in my way, so I think I may count on being a nice animal, something elegant and lively, with a love of fun. An otter, perhaps."

"Personally I think an otter life would be rather enjoyable," continued Laura; "salmon to eat all year round and the satisfaction of being able to catch trout in their own homes without having to wait for hours till they condescend to rise to the fly you've been dangling before them . . ."

"Think of the otter hounds," interposed Amanda; "how dreadful to be hunted down and then torn to pieces!"

"Rather fun with half the neighborhood watching, and anyhow not worse than this Saturday-to-Tuesday business of dying by inches; and then I shall go on to be something else. If I had been a moderately good otter I suppose I might come back as something a little closer to human form—a big brown baboon or something."

"I wish you would be serious," sighed Amanda. "You really ought to be if you're only going to live till Tuesday."

As a matter of fact Laura died on Monday.

"So dreadfully upsetting," Amanda complained to her uncle-in-law Sir Lulworth Quayne. "I'd already asked quite a lot of people down for golf and fishing, and the rhododendrons are just looking their best."

"Laura always was inconsiderate," commiserated Sir Lulworth.

"And she had the craziest ideas," said Amanda. "Do you know she believed that she would come back to life as an otter!"

"One meets with those ideas of reincarnation so frequently," said Sir Lulworth, "that one can hardly put them down as being crazy. And Laura was such an unaccountable person in this life that I should not like to lay down definite rules as to what she might do in an after state."

"You think she really might have passed into some animal form?" asked Amanda. She was one of those people who shape their opinions based on those around them.

Just then Egbert entered the breakfast room, wearing an air of bereavement that Laura's demise would have been insufficient, in itself, to account for.

"Four of my Sussex speckled hens have been killed," he exclaimed. "The

very four that were to go to the county fair on Friday. One of them was dragged away and eaten in the middle of that new carnation bed that I've been to so much trouble and expense over. My best flower bed and my best fowls singled out for destruction! It almost seems as if the brute that did the deed had special knowledge of how to be as devastating as possible in a short space of time."

"Was it a fox, do you think?" asked Amanda.

"Sounds more like a polecat," said Sir Lulworth.

"No," said Egbert, "there were marks of webbed feet all over the place, and we followed the tracks down to the stream at the bottom of the garden. It was an otter."

Amanda looked quickly and furtively at Sir Lulworth.

Egbert was too agitated to eat any breakfast and went out to supervise the strengthening of the poultry-yard fences.

"I think she might at least have waited for the funeral to be over," said Amanda in a scandalized voice.

"It's her funeral, you know," said Sir Lulworth. "It's a fine point in etiquette how far one ought to show respect to one's own mortal remains."

Disregard for mortuary convention was carried to further lengths the next day while the family was at the funeral and the remaining survivors of the Sussex speckled hens were massacred. The marauder's line of retreat seemed to have embraced most of the flower beds on the lawn, but the strawberry beds in the lower garden had also suffered.

"I shall get the otter hounds to come here at the earliest possible moment," said Egbert savagely.

"On no account! You can't dream of such a thing!" exclaimed Amanda. "I mean, it wouldn't do, so soon after a funeral in the house."

"It's a case of necessity," said Egbert. "Once an otter takes to that sort of thing, it won't stop."

"Perhaps it will go elsewhere now that there are no more chickens left," suggested Amanda.

"One would think you wanted to shield the beast," said Egbert.

But even Amanda's opposition weakened when, while the family was at church the following Sunday, the otter made its way into the house, raided half a salmon from the larder, and shredded it into scaly fragments on the Persian rug in Egbert's studio.

"We shall have it hiding under our beds and biting pieces out of our feet before long," fumed Egbert, and from what Amanda knew of this particular otter, she felt that the possibility was not a remote one.

It was Amanda's friend and neighbor, Aurora Burret, who brought her news of the day's "sport."

"Pity you weren't along; we had a good day. We found it at once in the pool just below your garden."

"Was it—killed?" asked Amanda.

"Yes. A fine she-otter. Your husband got rather badly bitten in trying to tail it. Poor beast, I felt quite sorry for it—it had such a human look in its eyes when it was killed. You'll call me silly, but do you know who the look reminded me of? My dear woman, what is the matter?"

When Amanda had recovered to a certain extent from her attack of

nervous prostration, Egbert took her on a tour of India to recuperate. Change of scene speedily brought about the desired recovery of health and mental balance. The escapades of an adventurous otter in search of a variation of diet were viewed in their proper light. Amanda's normal placid temperament reasserted itself. Even a hurricane of shouted curses, coming from her husband's dressing-room, in her husband's voice, but hardly his usual vocabulary, failed to disturb her serenity as she leisurely brushed her hair one evening at a Bombay hotel.

"What's the matter? What has happened?" she asked in amused curiosity.

"The beast has stolen my new camera! Wait till I catch you, you little—"

"What beast?" asked Amanda, suppressing a desire to laugh. Egbert's language was so hopelessly inadequate to express his outraged feelings.

"A big brown baboon," spluttered Egbert.

And now Amanda is seriously ill.

chapter IX

THE STATEMENT
OF RANDOLPH CARTER

ADAPTED FROM H. P. LOVECRAFT

Again I say, I do not know what has become of Harley Warren, though I think—almost hope—that he is in peaceful oblivion, if there be anywhere so blessed a thing. It is true that I have for five years been his closest friend, and a partial sharer of his terrible researches into the unknown. I will not deny, though my memory is uncertain and indistinct, that this witness of yours may have seen us together as he says, on the Gainsville turnpike, walking toward Big Cypress Swamp, at half past eleven on that awful night. That we bore electric lanterns, spades, and a curious coil of wire with attached instruments, I will even affirm; for these things all played a part in the single hideous scene which remains burned into my shaken recollection. But of what followed, and of the reason I was found alone and dazed on the edge of the swamp next morning, I must insist that I know nothing save what I have told you over and over again. You say to me that there is nothing in the swamp or near it which could form the setting of that frightful episode. I reply that I knew nothing beyond what I saw. Vision or nightmare it may have been—vision or nightmare I fervently hope it was—yet it is all that my mind retains of what took place in those shocking hours after we left the sight of men. And why Harley Warren did not return, he or his shade—or some nameless thing I cannot describe—alone can tell.

As I have said before, the weird studies of Harley Warren were well known to me, and to some extent shared by me. Of his vast collection of strange, rare books on forbidden subjects I have read all that are written in the languages of which I am master; but these are few as compared with those in languages I cannot understand. Most, I believe, are in Arabic; and the fiend-inspired book which brought on the end—the book which he carried in his pocket out of the world—was written in characters whose like I never saw elsewhere. Warren would never tell me just what was in that book. As to the nature of our studies—must I say again that I no longer retain full comprehension? It seems to me rather merciful that I do not, for they were terrible studies, which I pursued more through reluctant fascination than through actual inclination. Warren always dominated me, and sometimes I feared him. I remember how I shuddered at his facial expression on the night before the awful happening, when he talked so incessantly of his theory, why certain corpses never decay, but rest firm and fat in their tombs for a thousand years. But I do not fear him now, for I suspect that he has known horrors beyond my ken. Now I fear for him.

Once more I say that I have no clear idea of our object on that night. Certainly, it had much to do with something in the book which Warren carried with him—that ancient book in undecipherable characters which had come

to him from India a month before—but I swear I do not know what it was that we expected to find. Your witness says he saw us at half past eleven on the Gainsville pike, headed for Big Cypress Swamp. This is probably true, but I have no distinct memory of it. The picture seared into my soul is of one scene only, and the hour must have been long after midnight; for a waning crescent moon was high in the vaporous heavens.

The place was an ancient cemetery; so ancient that I trembled at the manifold signs of immemorial years. It was in a deep, damp hollow, overgrown with rank grass, moss, and curious creeping weeds, and filled with a vague stench which my idle fancy associated absurdly with rotting stone. On every hand were the signs of neglect and decrepitude, and I seemed haunted by the notion that Warren and I were the first living creatures to invade a lethal silence of centuries. Over the valley's rim a wan, waning crescent moon peered through the noisome vapors that seemed to emanate from unheard-of catacombs, and by its feeble, wavering beams I could distinguish a repellent array of antique slabs, urns, gravestones, and mausoleum facades; all crumbling, moss grown, and moisture stained, and partly concealed by the gross luxuriance of the unhealthy vegetation.

My first vivid impression of my own presence in this terrible necropolis concerns the act of pausing with Warren before a certain half-obliterated sepulcher and of throwing down some burdens which we seemed to have been carrying. I now observed that I had with me an electric lantern and two spades, whilst my companion was supplied with a similar lantern and a portable telephone outfit. No word was uttered, for the spot and the task seemed known

to us; and without delay we seized our spades and commenced to clear away the grass, weeds, and drifted earth from the flat, archaic mortuary. After uncovering the entire surface, which consisted of three immense granite slabs, we stepped back some distance to survey the charnel scene; and Warren appeared to make some mental calculations. Then he returned to the sepulcher, and using his spade as a lever, sought to pry up the slab lying nearest to a stony ruin which may have been a monument in its day. He did not succeed, and motioned to me to come to his assistance. Finally our combined strength loosened the stone, which we raised and tipped to one side.

The removal of the slab revealed a black aperture, from which rushed an effluence of miasmal gases so nauseous that we started back in horror. After an interval, however, we approached the pit again, and found the exhalations less unbearable. Our lanterns disclosed the top of a flight of stone steps, dripping with some detestable discharge of the inner earth, and bordered by moist walls encrusted with saltpeter. And now for the first time my memory records verbal discourse, Warren addressing me at length in his mellow tenor voice; a voice singularly unperturbed by our awesome surroundings.

"I'm sorry to have to ask you to stay on the surface," he said, "but it would be a crime to let anyone with your frail nerves go down there. You can't imagine, even from what you have read and from what I've told you, the things I shall have to see and do. It's fiendish work, Carter, and I doubt if any man without ironclad sensibilities could ever see it through and come up alive and sane. I don't wish to offend you, and heaven knows I'd be glad enough to have you with me; but the responsibility is in a certain sense mine, and I couldn't drag a bundle of nerves like you down to probable death or madness. I tell you, you can't imagine what the thing is really like! But I promise to keep you informed over the telephone of every move—you see I've enough wire here to reach to the center of the earth and back!"

I can still hear, in memory, those coolly spoken words; and I can still remember my remonstrances. I seemed desperately anxious to accompany my friend into those sepulchral depths, yet he proved inflexibly obdurate. At one time he threatened to abandon the expedition if I remained insistent; a threat which proved effective, since he alone held the key to the thing. All this I can still remember, though I no longer know what manner of thing we sought. After he had obtained my reluctant acquiescence in his design, Warren picked up the reel of wire and adjusted the instruments. At his nod I took one of the latter and seated myself upon an aged, discolored gravestone close by the newly uncovered aperture. Then he shook my hand, shouldered the coil of wire, and disappeared within that indescribable ossuary.

For a minute I kept sight of the glow of his lantern, and heard the rustle of the wire as he laid it down after him; but the glow soon disappeared abruptly, as if a turn in the stone staircase had been encountered, and the sound died away almost as quickly. I was alone, yet bound to the unknown depths by those magic strands whose insulated surface lay green beneath the struggling beams of that waning crescent moon.

I constantly consulted my watch by the light of my electric lantern, and listened with feverish anxiety at the receiver of the telephone; but for more than a quarter of an hour heard nothing. Then a faint clicking came from the instrument, and I called down to my friend in a tense voice. Apprehensive as I was, I was nevertheless unprepared for the words which came up from that uncanny vault in accents more alarmed and quivering than any I had heard before from Harley Warren. He, who had so calmly left me a little while previously, now called from below in a shaky whisper more portentous than the loudest shriek:

"God! If you could see what I am seeing!"

I could not answer. Speechless, I could only wait. Then came the frenzied tones again:

"Carter, it's terrible—monstrous—unbelievable!"

This time my voice did not fail me, and I poured into the transmitter a flood of excited questions. Terrified, I continued to repeat, "Warren, what is it? What is it?"

Once more came the voice of my friend, still hoarse with fear, and now apparently tinged with despair:

"I can't tell you, Carter! It's too utterly beyond thought—I dare not tell you—no man could know it and live—Great God! I never dreamed of this!"

Stillness again, save for my now incoherent torrent of shuddering inquiry. Then the voice of Warren in a pitch of wilder consternation:

"Carter! For the love of God, put back the slab and get out of this if you can! Quick!—leave everything else and make for the outside—it's your only chance! Do as I say, and don't ask me to explain!"

I heard, yet was able only to repeat my frantic questions. Around me were the tombs and the darkness and the shadows; below me, some peril beyond the radius of the human imagination. But my friend was in greater danger than I, and through my fear I felt a vague resentment that he should deem me capable of deserting him under such circumstances. More clicking, and after a pause a piteous cry from Warren:

"Beat it! For God's sake, put back the slab and beat it, Carter!"

Something in the boyish slang of my evidently stricken companion unleashed my faculties. I formed and shouted a resolution, "Warren, brace up! I'm coming down!" But at this offer the tone of my auditor changed to a scream of utter despair:

"Don't! You can't understand! It's too late—and my own fault. Put back the slab and run—there's nothing else you or anyone can do now!"

The tone changed again, this time acquiring a softer quality, as of hopeless resignation. Yet it remained tense through anxiety for me.

"Quick—before it's too late!"

I tried not to heed him; tried to break through the paralysis which held me, and to fulfill my vow to rush down to his aid. But his next whisper found me still held inert in the chains of stark horror.

"Carter—hurry! It's no use—you must go—better one than two—the slab—"

A pause, more clicking, then the faint voice of Warren:

"Nearly over now—don't make it harder—cover up those damned steps and run for your life—you're losing time—so long, Carter—won't see you again."

Here Warren's whisper swelled into a cry; a cry that gradually rose to a shriek fraught with all the horror of the ages—

"Curse these hellish things—legions—my God! Beat it! Beat it! BEAT IT!"

After that was silence. I know not how many interminable eons I sat stupefied; whispering, muttering, calling, screaming into that telephone. Over and over again through those eons I whispered and muttered, called, shouted, and screamed, "Warren! Warren! Answer me—are you there?"

And then there came to me the crowning horror of all—the unbelievable, unthinkable, almost unmentionable thing. I have said that eons seemed to elapse after Warren shrieked forth his last despairing warning, and that only my own cries now broke the hideous silence. But after a while there was a further clicking in the receiver, and I strained my ears to listen. Again I called down, "Warren, are you there?" and in answer heard the thing which has brought this cloud over my mind. I do not try, gentlemen, to account for that thing—that voice—nor can I venture to describe it in detail, since the first words took away my consciousness and created a mental blank which reaches to the time of my awakening in the hospital. Shall I say that the voice was deep; hollow; gelatinous; remote; unearthly; inhuman; disembodied? What shall I say? It was the end of my experience, and is the end of my story. I heard it, and knew no more—heard it as I sat petrified in that unknown cemetery in the hollow, amidst the crumbling stones and the falling tombs, the rank vegetation and the miasmal vapors—heard it well up from the innermost depths of that damnable open sepulcher as I watched amorphous, deathly shadows dance beneath an accursed waning moon.

And this is what it said:

"You fool, Warren is DEAD!"